THE
NORTH
OF GOD

THE NORTH OF GOD

STEVE STERN

MELVILLEHOUSE
BROOKLYN, NEW YORK

FOR HOWARD SCHWARTZ

PORTIONS OF THIS BOOK APPEARED IN ALTERED FORM IN THE
LITERARY JOURNAL *EPOCH*, AND IN *THE WEDDING JESTER*
(GRAYWOLF PRESS 1999).

BOOK DESIGN: BLAIR AND HAYES, BASED ON A SERIES DESIGN BY
DAVID KONOPKA

MELVILLE HOUSE PUBLISHING
145 PLYMOUTH STREET
BROOKLYN, NEW YORK 11201

WWW.MHPBOOKS.COM

FIRST MELVILLE HOUSE PRINTING: MAY 2008

LIBRARY OF CONGRESS CATALOGING-IN-PUBLICATION DATA

STERN, STEVE, 1947-
  THE NORTH OF GOD / STEVE STERN.
    P. CM.
  ISBN 978-1-933633-56-5 (PBK.)
1. HOLOCAUST, JEWISH (1939-1945)--FICTION. 2. JEWS--FIC-
TION. I. TITLE.
  PS3569.T414N67 2008
  813'.54--DC22

                              2008007030

THE NORTH OF GOD

YIDDISH TWILIGHT

Before he became a dissolute wanderer and corrupter of children, Hershel Khevreman was a devout student of Talmud. Son of an impoverished poulterer known as Itche Chicken in his Galician village of Zshldz, he'd far outdistanced the local scholars, and soon after his bar mitzvah had set off on foot in search of a higher learning, landing eventually in the court of the Saczer Rebbe in the remote Carpathian outpost of Stary Sacz. There, beyond the diseases and rampaging Cossacks that plagued his native Zshldz, beyond the reach of his dowdy parents, Hershel flourished; he earned a reputation for scholarship that in turn brought him to the attention of Reb Avrom Treklekh, a prosperous distiller of fruit kvass, who offered Hershel his daughter's hand in marriage. Despite his youth (he was barely sixteen) and his absorption in the study of the Law, Hershel was no fool, and he anxiously looked forward to assuming his portion as a rich man's son-in-law.

On the Monday night before the wedding (Tuesday weddings were considered propitious because God had said thrice "It is well" on the Third Day) Hershel and his fellow scholars were gathered in the *besmedresh* for an informal celebration. With its timeworn benches and sagging shelves of books, their weathered pages as scalloped as cockleshells, with its burbling samovar atop a barrel-shaped stove, the study house was more than a classroom; it was parlor, dining hall, and dormitory to the majority of yeshiva boys. Outside, the early autumn wind was indistinguishable from the howling of wolves on the heights above the town; while across the steppes below swept the armies of an emperor, a kaiser, and a czar, for whom the *zhids* were cannon fodder or target practice. Below their mountain fastness were blood libels and legal pogroms, a night distinctly unfriendly to the Jews; but despite (or because of) the dangers, the house of study remained for its occupants as snug as a humidor.

For the eve of Hershel's wedding, the scholars, penniless all, had nevertheless managed to stockpile some refreshment: a little herring, zweiback and sour pickles, a couple of bottles of shabbes wine. This they did more out of a sense of tradition than from any love of the groom, whom they largely considered an arrogant prig. If they had anything to celebrate, it was that the self-styled Talmud *chochem*, the wise guy, would soon be moving in under Reb Avrom's ample roof, and hopefully out of their hair. Still, unaccustomed to excess, the lads found themselves growing festive with drink, the friskier among them teasing the groom in a spirit that betrayed their jealousy.

Velvl Spfarb, for instance, a fat boy who fancied himself a serious challenger to Hershel's standing as resident genius, raised his glass to propose: "If the shekels are there, the groom will appear." Meant to suggest Hershel's mercenary intentions, it was a hypocritical dig, since who among them wouldn't have liked to be in the scholar's shoes? Then Shloyme Aba, ungainly in peaked cap and patched gaberdine, a permanent leer across his foxy face, went Velvl one better. "The uglier the piece, the luck will increase," he declared; because the truth was that Hershel's betrothed, Shifra Puah—Hershel had hardly noticed her at the contract-signing, so beguiled was he by the uncracked books in Reb Avrom's study—was not a very prepossessing young woman. In fact, just thirteen, with a body like an empty pillow slip and a pinched face the hue of a biscuit dipped in borscht, she was not a woman at all.

Seated stiffly in the place of honor at the head of a scored oak table, Hershel chafed at their disrespect. A proven prodigy who'd bested them all in the toe-to-toe *pilpul* discourse, he didn't like being used with such familiarity. Moreover, observing an obligatory pre-nuptial fast, the bridegroom was forbidden food and drink, which made it doubly hard to appreciate their sportive mood. Still Hershel reminded himself that, given the degree of good fortune that had lately befallen him, he could afford to be a little indulgent. After all, what did he want beyond the leisure to pursue a lifelong exploration of Mosaic Law? And if that pursuit were sustained by the generosity of in-laws in a house like a Venetian palazzo, then how manifold were his blessings; and how small a price to pay for them was the sniping of his less accomplished peers.

The drudge, Muni Misery, shoulders drooping from what he liked to claim was the weight of history, offered this observation: "A wedding is like a funeral but with musicians." He was seconded by Yukie Etka Zeidl's, ordinarily a taciturn oaf but moved to speak up tonight: "A man goes to the bridal canopy alive and returns a corpse." More proverbs equating marriage with death were tendered as toasts, after which the boys took another sip of wine.

Then Shloyme Aba, the closest to an authentic wag the yeshiva could boast of, bounded onto the table to pose a riddle like a wedding jester. "Why," he asked, extending a finger from the ragged wing of his sleeve, "does a stretcher have only two poles while a wedding canopy has four? Because—" He was interrupted before he could answer himself.

"Because, with a stretcher you bury only one person," it was Hershel, unable to suffer in silence any longer, "while with a wedding canopy you bury two." Risen to his feet, he displayed the assurance that made him both the bane and envy of the other students.

There was a hush while the gathering fumbled for some common attitude toward Hershel's intrusion, though none were perhaps more surprised than the bridegroom himself. Had he, by participating, given his blessing to these unseemly goings on? An asthmatic wheeze from Shloyme Aba signaled the others that the guest of honor had at last entered into the spirit of the occasion; raising his glass, he proposed another toast, this one more or less sincere. "God send you the wife you deserve!" Hershel, at some expense of dignity, forced a smile.

As the company joined in the toast, Shloyme Aba hopped down from the table and launched into an impersonation of their teacher, Rabbi Asher ben Yedvab, the Saczer Rebbe. Rattle-boned, with a nose like a spigot, Shloyme was eminently suited for the role. He bent his back, fluttered an eyelid, fidgetting a mock-palsied hand at the level of his crotch; while Velvl Spfarb, who'd done yeoman service in assisting the actual rebbe, stepped forward to lend his support to the sham. The hammer-headed Salo Pinkas took Shloyme Aba's other arm.

"P-place a drop of blood on the t-tip of a sword," he intoned in the rebbe's reedy stammer. "The instant it t-t-takes the drop to d-duh-duhhh [Salo Pinkas slapped him hard on the back] to divide into two parts, that is t-twilight."

It was a fair approximation of the Saczer's fanciful pronouncements, and the students cackled their approval. Goaded by the laughter, Shloyme Aba further exaggerated the rebbe's galvanic tics and spasms, joggling so that his supporters could barely hold on.

Then he turned toward the eastern wall of the study house, where a ponderous piece of mahogany furniture stood. This was the hall tree the rebbe had brought with him on his journey from Przemysl over half a century before. Since the study house had no vestibule and the thing itself looked nothing like a tree—was in fact a tall, throne-like structure with a seat and a large oval mirror circumscribed by coathooks—it was a constant source of amusement to the yeshiva boys. Especially amusing to them was their otherwise ascetic rebbe's attachment to his hall tree. He addressed it with a reverence typically reserved for the ark in the synagogue, wherein the scrolls of the Law were kept. This made Shloyme Aba's prayerful convulsions, body flapping like a shutter in a gale, all the more risible to his audience.

Even the haughty bridegroom succumbed to the comedy, which, fueled by drink and the zeal of his fellows, wildly exceeded Shloyme Aba's ordinary mischief. Having stooped to make an adjustment, he now turned back around to show a limp sock dangling from his fly—unbuttoned flies being one of the rebbe's frequent oversights.

"Rabbi Ishmael ben Yose's member was the size of a wineskin of nine *k–k–k–kav*," he proclaimed. "But Rav Papa himself had a shwantz like the b-baskets of Hip-hip-areenum . . ."

While most still hooted their encouragement, some of the younger boys had fallen silent, perhaps sensing that Shloyme Aba had crossed a line. Hershel, who for his part had never shared the others' unconditional affection for their rebbe, applauded the imposture. He had always been irritated by Rabbi ben Yedvab's overheated romance with Torah, an attitude he deemed lacking decorum and courting indecency. ("Like the s-sex of the gazelle is the Torah," the rebbe was wont to say, "for whose husband every t-t-time is like the first.") He disapproved of how the old *tzadik* used scripture as a stimulus to ecstatic transports. If scripture was meant to be a stimulus for anything, thought Hershel, it was to inspire practical interpretations, such as Maimonides' *Mishneh Torah* or Rashi's commentaries—texts the scholar tended to prefer to the Pentateuch itself.

So when Shloyme Aba, whose performance was approaching the feverish, began reciting the betrothal benedictions, Hershel—reasoning that the burlesque was after all in the nature of a rehearsal—stepped up beside him. Velvl Spfarb, as if seized by conscience, backed furtively away, but Yukie Etka Zeidl's took his place, and together he and Salo Pinkas, in lieu of a wedding canopy, raised a threadbare caftan over the bridegroom's head. "*Mi adir al ha-kol* b-b-biddle-bum . . ." chanted Shloyme Aba, having faced the hall tree again; as over his shoulder Hershel took the measure of himself in the cloudy mirror. With his interest generally fixed on the abstract, the prodigy had seldom concerned himself with appearances—why should he care what kind of figure he cut in the tortured alleys of Stary Sacz? But tonight, no doubt infected by the high spirits of his companions (he hadn't thought of them as "companions" until tonight), Hershel felt peculiarly at home in his body, and noted that he wasn't a bad looking chap. Slender as a taper, he stood remarkably straight for a boy who spent his days bent over books. His cheeks, still beardless, were unblemished by the eruptions afflicting so many other students; his nose was imperially aquiline. Ginger curls boiled from under his skullcap; his earlocks were like scrolled ribbons, his eyes echoing the emerald of the mirror glass. All in all, Hershel thought he made quite an affecting bridegroom.

As Shloyme Aba completed the nuptial formula, Muni Misery, never so antic, placed a goblet near Hershel's foot for him to stomp. A stickler for protocol, however, Hershel came suddenly back to himself.

"How can I crush the glass," he wanted to know, "before I put the ring on the finger of my betrothed?"

The question was calculated to abort the ceremony, which to Hershel's mind had gone far enough; and since he was confident that the ring remained in the safekeeping of his future father-in-law until tomorrow, he assumed the horseplay was at an end. But Muni Misery again rose to the challenge. He presented Hershel with a loop he'd fashioned from a tuft of fur belonging to the perpetually molting study house cat. (A brindled and querulous animal whom the rebbe suspected of being the reincarnation of Menachem Mendl of Kotzk.) Hershel, for whom the charade was effectively over, received the loop a little impatiently, but having committed himself thus far, he accepted his cue to proceed. He began to recite, albeit half-heartedly, the sacred *qiddushin*: "*Harai at mekudeshet lee, b'ta-ba-at-zu, k'dat Moshe v'Yisrael.* Be sanctified to me with this ring in accordance with the law of Moses and Israel." Then he placed the loop over the crooked brass finger of a coathook.

The boldness of the gesture made him shudder, the shudder reverberating around the room—because no sooner had the ring encircled the coathook than the surface of the mirror began to stir.

Hershel wondered if the vinous breaths of the other *bochers* had distorted his own perception, inducing a dizziness that blurred his image in the glass. He momentarily lost his balance, stepping on the goblet which made a sound like a jaw munching bone; but more fascinated than frightened, he steadied himself, observing how the rippling glass resembled watered silk in a breeze. He watched his image begin to fragment and dissolve in the murky oval—as if a reflection on a pond were being replaced by a body floating to the surface. Then the body acquired dimensions that contradicted the flat face of the mirror, assuming the form of a young woman, tall and lean, with billowing midnight hair. She was wearing a loose cambric shift that clung to her sinewy limbs as she stepped from the mirror onto the swept clay floor.

With the exception of Menachem Mendl, screeching as he arched his back, screeching louder as he singed his fur on the stove, no one had the wit to utter a sound. Taking flight, they climbed over one another in their frantic efforts to escape through the solitary door. The sluefooted Yukie Etka Zeidl's stumbled at the threshold and was trodden upon by his cronies; Velvl Spfarb, already backed against the far wall, squeezed his girth through a narrow casement and tumbled out head first. Hershel himself would doubtless have been in their number, had not the woman—she seemed for all practical purposes a woman, of about eighteen in human years—had she not taken his hand in her own, which was brackish and cold.

"My pretty husband," she said, her voice as tart as prune compote, "*shalom*."

Your garden variety yeshiva scholar was never known for his discretion. So routine were his days that the least irregularity—one fainted from hunger, another suffered a nocturnal discharge—was likely to trigger a rash of *loshen horeh*, of gossip. Any deviation from the usual was subject to scrupulous inquiry; this was their habit. But what the boys had witnessed in the study house tonight so far surpassed their tolerance for abnormality that it confounded their ability to carry tales. Too prodigious and frightful a burden to pass on, this one was better left alone.

The few who boarded in town fled to their hosts; the rest sought sanctuary across the compound in the little stone shul. Despite the protests of Fishke the shammes, who reminded them that the small hours were reserved for the dead, they insisted on saying penitential prayers. Most remained in the synagogue—its haunted atmosphere notwithstanding—throughout the night, though some, more curious than chastened, girded themselves to return to the *besmedresh*. There they found Hershel Khevreman naked but for his ritual garment, huddled on the seat of the hall tree with unfocussed eyes.

Nobody dared to interrogate him, nor did Hershel, absently accepting his trousers from one, his waistcoat from another, offer any enlightenment. He said nothing to counter their unspoken pact to forget this evening's incident altogether. Only Velvl Spfarb, who'd turned around after diving through the window and lost his smugness for all time—only he reported the story, first to the rebbe and again many years later, after Hershel himself had long since passed into legend. Then Velvl told how the paralyzed scholar had submitted to the woman's toying with his ritual fringes, her unfastening of his suspender buttons, the stroking of his chest; how she'd hunched her shoulders to let the shift slither down her tawny length, pooling like fog at her feet; after which they'd admired each other in the glass. And when, having touched the mirror to no purpose, Hershel turned to touch her umber flesh, she let loose a cry—like a sound that had traveled through three twists of a devil's shofar to rattle the study house walls.

(The "three twists" were a bit of embroidery Velvl permitted himself despite the families who reproached him for recounting such an unsavory tale. Already sick with fear in a crowded boxcar clattering toward *Gehinnom*, why should their children be further abused by the phantoms of a windy old man?)

When they'd expended enough guilty solicitude on him, the students nudged Hershel out the door, pointing him in the direction of the clockmaker's shop where he boarded. Tottering through the switchback streets of the Jewish quarter, the prodigy attempted to apply his talmudic logic to what had transpired, but found that once reliable faculty in sad disrepair.

With a borrowed key he entered the shuttered shop, its interior as alive with ticking as a field of locusts. Last week had been Kalman Tsensifer the blacksmith and his ringing anvil, the week before Falik the cobbler and his last; this week was Yosl Berg the clockmaker with his ticking, his wife with the swinging pendulum of her broom. Thus did the *shtetl* keep time with a pleasing monotony to the rhythm of Hershel's days. Parting a curtain, he slipped into the close compartment that served as parlor, kitchen, and bedroom for the Bergs. He crossed the floor, his footsteps muted by the clocks and the stormy snoring from behind a burlap screen, then climbed a short ladder to the loft above the ceramic tile stove. There, amid the risen odors of goose fat and human gas, he stripped to the flannel *gatkes* (it was cold for the month of Tishri) and crawled into the quilted cavern of his featherbed.

Raised on mealy potatoes by a lumpish mother, herself potato-shaped, and a father festooned in feathers like a flightless bird, Hershel had conceived, since coming to Stary Sacz, a fondness for creature comforts. He liked clean linen, warm rooms, and bakery goods. In fact, his affection for featherbeds might rival on occasion his passion for the conundrums of the Law. But such pleasures marked the limits of Hershel's indulgence. The wayward thoughts and temptations the rebbe described as the reverse side of the scholarly virtues seldom disturbed him. To resolve some thorny legal problem—the culpability, say, of a family into whose home a mouse brings unleavened crumbs on Passover; or how much farther to rend a garment upon the death of a near relation than of a friend—this was meat and drink to Hershel; of the commentaries of the oral Torah, he could say along with the psalmist: "How sweet are Thy words unto my palate!" Nothing in the larders of the households on whose charity he depended had ever beckoned him more.

But all that was changed in an hour by a lady who stepped out of a mirror—which was of course impossible. It was a phenomenon that defied the rational categories, a thing that would never have been credited in the pandects of Maimonides or the Vilna Gaon. The Jews of Stary Sacz, *hasids* and *mitnagdim* alike, might be prone in their unworldly isolation to superstition. They might observe their watchnights, shooing demons from a baby's crib on the eve of his *bris*, incanting in the chambers of women in labor: "Womb, lie down!" But Hershel Khevreman, who had no patience with magic, discounted all irrational expressions of faith. He discounted them so fervently that he sometimes wondered if faith itself were not irrational. Wasn't God, when you thought of it, a somewhat absurd proposition? This was a line of reasoning Hershel rarely followed any further, always returning to a conscientious exegeses of texts. Study, that was his ruling impulse, overruled though it had been tonight.

So where had she fled to? For as soon as the boys began to creep back into the study house, she was gone, leaving him to crumple in a heap against the hall tree.

To ask himself again if she were real was to belabor the question, for hadn't he already dismissed her as a figment, a dream—though it's said that "A dream is one-sixtieth of prophecy," and this one he recalled with uncommon lucidity. There were, for instance, all the things she had which, *l'havdil*, he did not: such as the hair in its abundant black whorls that could founder a frigate, the nipples that stood to attention with a look, the fluted ribs, the close-pored hollow where her navel should have been, her laughter like a glockenspiel . . .

According to the rebbe's precious Kabbalah, of which Hershel was deeply skeptical, one must yield to sin before attaining the higher status of penitent. But Hershel had argued from tractate Berakhot that "At the place reserved for penitents, no righteous man may stand," and surely he, by virtue of diligent study, was a righteous man. So what was he thinking? Only that, real or not, the lady from the mirror had awakened in him a desire that—God forbid!—he would trade Shifrah Puah and all the bounty that came with her to realize.

Then it occurred to Hershel the only logical explanation for what had taken place tonight was that he'd lost his mind. Coincidental with this conclusion the ladder creaked; it creaked once, twice, the planks giving gently, a body with a pungent odor (its flesh mingling fire and ice) sliding next to him in his goosedown cocoon.

"My man," her breath kindled his brain like an ember in a warming pan, "we got yet unfinished business . . ."

Around the same time the old bachelor rebbe, Asher ben Yedvab, was awakened by a knocking at the door of his cottage adjoining the *besmedresh*. Wearing only his nightshirt and *talis koton*, a shawl pulled over his scurfy head, he allowed himself to be tugged by an excited Velvl Spfarb into the study house. There he detached himself from the gibbering student and proceeded in his jerking progress—elbow, pelvis, and knee each attempting to go its own way—toward the hall tree. With the cat twined fretfully about his ankle, the Saczer struggled to maintain his balance as he inspected his trophy. He removed the loop of fur from the coathook, held it a moment in his twitching palm, and smacked his bearded face, leaving the loop stuck in his eye like a monocle. Then he peered into the mirror whose surface had cleared of mist, which permitted him to see straight through to the other side.

"Come down, Hershel Khevreman!" Reb Yosl summoned from below. "The *kloger* rattled the shutter already. Would you be late for morning prayers on your wedding day?"

Torpid from too little sleep, Hershel opened a bleary eye, letting the phrase "wedding day" resonate sweetly in his head. He yawned luxuriously, stretched, extending his left arm from beneath the quilting, and endeavored to stretch his right—which was pinned beneath a breathing form. "Oy!" he cried, starting up from the pallet in consternation, as a hand gently squeezed him between the legs. He made a grab for the hand, and found there instead the warm head that had slid from his chest to burrow in his lap. Hershel wondered a panicked instant if he were giving birth.

"What's the matter?" called the clockmaker.

"Nothing!" Hershel chirped. "I banged my head on a rafter."

Rigid as the carved wooden figures that hourly emerged from the face of his clocks, Reb Yosl told him to hurry it up, he moved like a fart in brine.

"Go ahead," stalled Hershel, the hand having abandoned its hold to a pair of moist lips, "I'll catch up with you."

"Basha Reba," Yosl protested to his wife, who seldom spoke; though the fragrance of the tea she was brewing caused the prodigy's stomach to churn. Despite the circumstances, he still remembered that he was hungry; all his appetites, it seemed, were wide awake. "Basha Reba," complained the clockmaker, "it's a sluggard we got under our roof. Reb Sluggard, come down, you'll start your honeymoon tomorrow."

"Dawhahefing," said the voice from beneath the covers with her mouth full. ("That's what he thinks.") Her hair filled the scholar's lap like spilled lokshen noodles, her mumbling jaw made him whimper aloud.

"What's that?" asked Reb Yosl. "Basha Reba, what's he saying?"

"I'm coming!" cried Hershel with more emphasis than the situation called for, commanding all the heartsunk strength he had left to pry himself free.

He swarmed down the ladder still pulling his pants on, prompting the clockmaker's wife (who disapproved of young men on principle) to throw her apron over her vinegar face. Her husband squinted in puzzlement through cockeyed spectacles, suggesting "*Shpilkes?*" as their boarder bolted past him for the door.

If he'd hoped to lose himself among the felt caps and gaberdines crowded into the study house for the morning service, Hershel was soon disabused of the notion. Already distinguished for his status as *khasn*, bridegroom, he was made even more conspicuous by the presence of his prospective father-in-law. Chief elector of the merchants' synagogue—the ornate cedar pile behind the market platz—Reb Avrom had condescended, for the *khasn*'s sake, to pray this morning among Rabbi ben Yedvab's hasidim. For their part the hasids, devoted consumers of Reb Avrom's merchandise, fawningly acknowledged the honor. Throughout their semi-silent articles of faith, they winked at the bandy distiller, expressing their shared amusement at the bridegroom's nervousness.

They snickered at how Hershel had managed to entangle himself in his own phylacteries, as if—he feared—they could read his mind. Perhaps they perceived that, fatigued and famished from his unending fast, aching in every part, he was helplessly reliving the episode of the night before: when, after the first great wave of passion had subsided, he'd wished her gone. And when she refused to leave him, somewhat heartened by the unbroken snoring from the householders below, he'd summoned the courage to ask her, "Who are you?"

"I'm the black *neshomeh*, the soul below the belt," she whispered, a sulphur moon through the dormer aglint in her teasing eye, "I'm the naughty intention. Three groschen worth of asafetida I can eat on an empty stomach without losing my skin. Take a chalice from the smithy, fill it with pomegranate seeds, circle it with roses and set it in the sun, and you got only an inkling of my beauty . . ."

Then she said she wasn't a woman at all but a succubus, a daughter of the demon Lilith named Salka, who'd been trapped in the mirror over half a century. This was owing to a spell invoked by none other than the Saczer Rebbe himself, with whom she'd attempted to interfere during his own student days. But unlike Hershel he'd resisted her charms. He'd tricked her into admiring herself in the mirror of a hall tree in the home of the wealthy merchant where he took his meals. Then he'd uttered a swift incantation and *presto*! Salka found herself confined to the other side of the glass. But rather than abandon the hall tree, the young rabbi had purchased it, over his host's insistence that he accept it as a gift: let it be included as part of the dowry attached to the merchant's unwed daughter. But the youth, who'd developed a twitching that rendered him incompatible with domestic tranquility, took the hall tree instead of the girl; he lugged it over the mountains from Przemysl to Stary Sacz, where he installed it in a prominent place in his "court."

"And that's where I waited for you to release me, my fated one," said the succubus, nibbling the lobe of Hershel's ear.

He'd wanted to prove he was done with her, that his will was as strong as any apprentice *tzadik*'s; he wanted to disbelieve in her altogether—but he'd nevertheless responded to her touch with a blind urgency. And now, as Hershel watched the Saczer davening fitfully on the dais, his torso like a runaway metronome, he wondered why he should feel so jealous of such a comical old man.

After prayers the men dispersed, causing Hershel further annoyance with their conspiratorial pinches and backslaps. Reb Avrom, distributing *noblesse oblige* left and right as he departed, paused to chuck the prodigy's chin. "Torah is the best of wares," he announced, as if bestowing sound business advice. Then, while the room reverted back to a yeshiva, the boys, saying hasty blessings over milk-boiled groats before pairing off to pursue their studies, each stole private glances at the bridegroom. To avoid their scrutiny, Hershel took a seat at the end of a bench and buried his head in a volume of Talmud.

"If a fledgling bird is found within fifty cubits of a dovecote," he read, hoping to solace himself in the old familiar way, "it belongs to the owner of the dovecote. If it is found outside the limit of fifty cubits, it belongs to the person that finds it. But Rabbi Jeremiah asked: If one foot of the fledgling is within the limit of fifty cubits, and one foot is outside it, what is the law?"

Hershel thought the question unbelievably stupid. Clamorous dialogues were developing all around him; children ushered into the study house by the *melammed* had begun reciting their *alef-bais* to the beat of his leather knout. Again Hershel addressed the text, trying to decipher it with a speed that outran his critical judgment, let alone his gnawing anxieties. Had Basha Reba discovered the creature in the loft and run shrieking into the street? Salka was nothing if not elusive, but she was also unpredictable, a quality he admired at the risk (he supposed) of his immortal soul. Unable to concentrate, Hershel asked himself when had he ever before been unable to concentrate.

Then a shadow fell across the page and Rabbi ben Yedvab, supported in his quivering by an abject Velvl Spfarb, stood before him. Hershel was aware of being the object of all eyes.

"I see your t-text is the B-b-bava Batra," said the tzadik, his facial tics signaling the commencement of a standard catechism. "So tell me what three things ch-ch-ch-changed in the days of Enosh b-ben Seth?"

Hershel began his response with characteristic aplomb: "Corpses putrefied, men's faces turned apelike, and . . ." he faltered. Was it possible that his memory had lost its steeltrap fidelity overnight?

"D-demons," reminded the rebbe, with alternately blinking eyes, "demons became free to work their will upon them. Hershel, it's your wed-d-ding-ding [Velvl dutifully swatted him on the back] your wedding day. You should visit the bathhouse."

Hershel straightened in his seat, wondering if his teacher, remarkable for his own rancid odor, could smell her salty essence on his person. Of course it was customary for a *khasn* to visit the bathhouse, not for purification—that was the bride's imperative—

but to prepare himself through meditating on the estate he was about to enter. Still, he was distrustful, feeling almost belligerent toward the wintry old man, his shifting features as difficult to read as a map in a storm. Also, while tradition demanded that the groom not be left alone on the day of his marriage, was such a mob of attendants really necessary? Most of the key participants from last night's burlesque—Shloyme Aba, Salo Pinkas, Muni Misery—had zealously volunteered to accompany Hershel, and waited for him now with the air of hired strongarms.

But having apparently no choice in the matter, Hershel rose and delivered himself up to his chaperones, resenting them nearly as much as he hoped they would stick by his side.

The bathhouse stood at the end of the butchers' shambles, its roof slates sprouting tussocks, its fissured brick walls breathing steam like a sleeping dragon. Serving on odd days as a *mikveh* for ritual immersion, the decrepit building was presided over by Moshe Cheesecloth—so-called for a skin condition resulting from his years of exposure to the sodden environment. It was to Moshe's good offices that the boys handed over the bridegroom, reluctant now to leave his protectors. Hershel also worried that the attendant might find, in checking his body for *shmutz*, marks left there by the talons of a lady demon. Never especially thorough, however, Moshe was too busy measuring the level of his rainwater cistern, fanning the copper furnace with a rawhide bellows, to make anything but a cursory inspection of Hershel's fingernails. Then he issued the scholar soap and towel, a birch broom to flog himself with, and sent him into the dressing cubicle off the entry.

Naked beneath the towel wrapped about his shoulders, Hershel padded into the humid tub room. He skirted a stack of smoldering rocks and, shedding the towel, lowered himself from the slippery platform into tepid, chest-deep water. He stirred the bilious green pool (in accordance with the precept against viewing one's own parts) and chased from his mind the water's resemblance to the surface of a certain looking-glass. Then leaning against the mossgrown tiles, he allowed himself a sigh. Gone for the moment was his apprehension at being left alone, the events of the night before having again withdrawn to the distance of dream. This was weariness, of course, but with it came a resurgence of hope regarding his imminent marriage. He had the feeling he might be only a short nap away from the knowledge that his future was yet in place. Yawning, Hershel turned to climb out of the tub and collapse on one of the cots that lined the walls, when a hand took hold of his ankle and dragged him under.

He fought his way sputtering back to the surface, taking deep gulps of the muggy air, frantically rubbing open his stinging eyes: to find her also risen from the turbulent pool, lit by an amber shaft from the bullseye window overhead. Her damp hair was strewn like a cat-o'-nine-tails across her laughing face, her coral-tipped breasts jigglingly upheld by the water. It was unconscionable that she should have appeared in broad daylight, however clouded in vapor. Clapping his hands over his face, Hershel recited the pertinent passage from the Shulkhan Arukh: "Semen-is-the-vitality-of-a-man's-body-and-when-it-issues-in-abundance-the-body-ages-the-strength-ebbs-the-eyes-grow-dim-the-breath-foul-the-hair-of-the-head-lashes-and-brows-fall-out . . ."

When he peeked through his fingers, she submitted in a voice whose music thrummed his vitals, "Did I tell you that Salka is short for *rusalka*, a mermaid?"

"For God's sake," pleaded Hershel, "will you leave . . .," forcing a whisper that was half a shriek, ". . . will you leave me alone!" Her presence in the *mikveh* was an affront to all things sacred, a violation of every law on the books.

Salka gave a careless shrug and began to pull herself out of the pool, the sleek, elongated *S* of her spine like a stem to the onion bulb of her glistening tush. Hershel wanted to tell her, "Demon, good riddance!", but a dreadful longing choked the words in his throat. Groaning, he threw his arms around her waist and squeezed mightily, hauling Salka back into the clammy water. He covered her with kisses so voracious that he felt they must constitute an untimely breaking of his fast, not that it mattered to a soul so already lost. A blessing came to his lips: "Praise God who permits the forbidden!", which was the phrase once invoked by the false prophet Sabbatai Zvi to excuse his sins. Afterwards Hershel couldn't remember whether they'd made love above or below the surface of the bath.

Outside, the bracing autumn breeze, laced with a bouquet from the slaughter yards, did nothing to lift the weight from his spirit. Weak-kneed and shame-faced, Hershel fell in among the ranks of his waiting comrades, but felt no safety in their numbers. Why, if sent by their teacher to guard the groom against his evil impulse—for how else explain their presence?—Why had they even bothered to respect his privacy? Why hadn't they charged into the bathhouse, interrupting what he would never have forgiven them for? And to think that only yesterday Hershel Khevreman had been a master of logic. Yesterday all he'd needed to complete his contentment—the dowry of a rich man's daughter—was in easy reach; now the distance between himself and his wedding lay before him like a no-man's-land he feared to cross alone.

Huddled around by bodyguards, he nonetheless felt dangerously exposed. As they straggled across the open expanse of the market square, raucous with vendors hawking dried fish and caged foul, Hershel wanted to take shelter in some obscure commentary. A virtual orphan since leaving Zshldze, he reasserted under his breath his credo that the Book was his home, its many branches his family tree; Rashi, Nachmanides, the Rambam—these were his real *mishpocheh*, the only company in which he felt truly secure. Then a glance beyond the academy caps of his fellows, and Hershel was granted a sight that made him shrink even further, retracting his neck into his shoulders turtle-style.

For over the way Reb Avrom's road-muddied Panhard touring car, complete with liveried chauffeur, had pulled up before the limewashed façade of Berel Schnapser's inn. In the backseat were a pair of passengers: one a scarecrow in an undersized rug coat dusted in feathers, the other a stolid, potato-shaped woman holding a carpet bag. Hershel recalled how, at the contract-signing, Reb Avrom had offered to bring them to town for the wedding, but the groom had argued that his parents didn't travel well. "Nonsense!" replied the distiller, who couldn't do enough for the boy whose scholarship guaranteed his in-laws a share in Kingdom Come. And while he knew he couldn't postpone the meeting indefinitely, Hershel figured his afflicted conscience would scarcely register another offense: so for the present he gave Itche Chicken and wife a wide berth.

In the meantime, too depleted to do otherwise, he surrendered himself wholesale to the custody of his peers. They in turn saw to it that the scholar remained upright through afternoon prayers, then—though he reached for a scriptural codex like a drowning man— hustled him off to be outfitted for the ceremony. Practically asleep on his feet, Hershel was conducted by a growing convoy of students through streets thick with the aromas of baking kugel and potted meat. The entire quarter, it seemed, was busy making dishes for the nuptial feast, while the youth on whose behalf they labored swooned from hunger, begging his beleaguered senses to let him be.

His escort, on the other hand, seemed to have recovered something of their mood of the night before. Putting aside their watchful solemnity, they grew livelier as the hour approached. They were jaunty as they marched the bridegroom through Reb Yosl's tiny shop, which (as Shloyme Aba observed) ticked like an anarchist's basement in Lodz. In the apartment behind the shop they twitted Basha Reba on the scythe-like movement of her broom; a few made as if to steal the almond torte left cooling on an upended washtub, while the rest led Hershel behind the fabric screen. There they attired him—Salo Pinkas holding him erect while Shloyme Aba and Yukie Zeidl's manipulated his arms and legs—in the silk plus-fours and ankle-length black *kittl* that the distiller had provided. They crowned him with the beaver-trimmed turban and drew him around to face a tarnished pierglass to admire his finery, but having lately conceived a phobia of mirrors, the groom turned his head.

It was left for Muni Misery to describe what he was missing with a philosophical wistfulness: "All grooms are handsome, all the dead are holy," he said, prompting Hershel to steal a sidelong look. What he saw resembled a folded parasol, its tip spearing a wheel of cheese gone furry with mold. But so relieved was he to find himself alone in the mirror that his nerves relaxed their grip on his insides, and he had abruptly to excuse himself.

In the yard in back of the shop he pulled to the latchless door of the privy; he raised the stiff garment, dropped his breeches, and plunked his bare bottom on the splintered wooden seat. Given his empty stomach, Hershel wondered what was left to purge, unless— settling himself for a restful interlude—he might look forward to the emptying of his unquiet mind. Then the door swung open and the succubus swept in, lifting her shift to straddle Hershel's naked knees, entwining his tongue with her viperish own.

"Mmphlmph!" protested Hershel, fighting to retrieve his face. "Please, Salka, not here!" It was all so unspeakably degrading.

But the creature rocked her hips as if in a *shukeling* prayer—and despite his exhaustion and the fetid surroundings, despite everything he'd previously deemed to be decent, the scholar responded to her beckoning movements. For some moments he clung to her, sucking the pastille of a nipple through the thin cambric bodice, anticipating as best he could her fluid rhythm; until, with a cry that was equal parts rapture and shame, Hershel let go, experiencing a seismic release both fore and aft. Then slumped in humiliation against the still heaving torso of the demoness, he wept guilty tears.

"Such an emotional boy," she breathlessly rebuked him, reaching for a cob from the pile on the floor: "Here, let me help you."

That's when Hershel heard the music, and once he'd determined that it originated on earth, that it came in fact from the street in front of the shop, he thought it might yet herald his salvation. Heedless of personal hygiene, he got to his feet, causing Salka to slide sprawling from his lap onto the spongy boards. "Impetuous!" she accused him even as he stumbled over her, snatched up his pants from around his ankles and staggered out to join the parade.

The groom's procession, led by one-half of Reb Dovidl Fiddle's klezmer ensemble, wound its way into the unpaved yard behind the hasids' listing stone shul. Though the date had been favorably fixed between the Days of Awe and Sukkot, it was late in the season for outdoor weddings. A brisk (if fair) afternoon, it would be nippy in the shaded court toward sunset. But bonfires would be lit to reduce the chill and—along with the garlands of garlic brandished by the guests—frighten the *sheydim*, the demons, away.

Ill-smelling and nearly insensible, jerked between the rebbe's dancing disciples (who'd hooked their arms through his), Hershel reminded himself he didn't believe in demons.

A path opened up for them through the crush of guests surrounding the canopy erected on four slender poles. In this way Hershel was made to run a gauntlet of *shtetl* society, from the crutched beggars on the periphery through the artisans, students, and hasidim, to the *machetonim*, the in-laws, seated just outside the *chupeh* in straight-backed chairs. Among the in-laws (sitting together but for the aisle dividing men from women) were the bridegroom's own parents, whom Hershel hadn't seen face-to-face in almost three years. He acknowledged them now with what little filial deference he had left: a polite bow; and they returned his greeting with stony, befuddled nods, clearly uncertain of why they'd been asked to come. Hershel waited for the embarrassment to set in, and for the remorse that followed embarrassment, but the pair of rustics seated before him were strangers, people of the chicken and distaff, not the Book. They had no real connection to the prodigy about to make a brilliant match with a rich man's daughter; and for all his debilitation Hershel felt reassured.

He took in for the first time the magnitude of the gathering, indicative of the wedding's great significance; he remarked the string of lanterns, the trestle tables awaiting platters of stuffed goose necks, the cauldrons of golden soup and calves' brain puddings as large as drums. Neither ghosts from the past nor the nightmares of a treacherous present, he concluded, could lay claim to him here, safe in the bosom of his community.

Opposite Hershel his erstwhile teacher, the Saczer Rebbe, had already begun his desultory benedictions, every feature of his face asserting its independence. Leaning on the humble arm of Velvl Spfarb, he nodded to the bridegroom, also bolstered by attendants, so that the two of them teetered like pugilists in a ring. Then came another flourish of fiddles and horns, as the other half of Reb Dovidl's orchestra ushered the bride's entourage into the compound. Flanked by her maids of honor, the *kallah*, the bride, came forward enshrouded in silk and brocade, her face mercifully concealed by a veil. Her venerable parents sashayed just behind.

When the bride had taken her place next to her intended, the music ceased and the rebbe curtailed his prayer. The guests shushed one another, as Rabbi ben Yedvab, his ceremonial sable as motheaten as his beard, was helped forward to perform the ritual lifting of the veil. Here was a moment Hershel had not looked forward to, when the *kallah*'s face would be revealed for his eyes only; for although entitled to call off the marriage if the face displeased him, he knew perfectly well what he must do: he must give his unqualified approval to the mousy, pinched *ponim* of Reb Avrom's daughter.

But the face beneath the mignonette veil, which the rebbe raised like the lid of a covered dish, bore small resemblance (if memory served) to Shifrah Puah's. This one stunned Hershel with its narrowed onyx eyes and kittenish grin, the sooty ringlets spilling from under her pumpernickel loaf of a wig. Then the veil was lowered again, though not before the succubus had taken the opportunity to wink.

Involuntarily Hershel winked back, satisfied that he must be hallucinating. Fine, he thought, let it be *her*: then last night's unholy wedding would be consecrated before Israel and all set right in the eyes of God. A shudder wracked Hershel's frame as he woke up to what he was thinking: he was contemplating his final disgrace, the mortal blow. The rebbe chanted the betrothal benedictions ("Who is m-m-mighty over all . . . ?"), and Hershel told himself this was the authentic piety—the kind that scourged the devils that haunted the *mikvehs* and privies but would never, in any case, dare to venture in public. But despite his wishful silent endorsement, Hershel still thought the rebbe's performance less convincing than Shloyme Aba's spoof of the night before.

Then a commotion was heard from the courtyard, and all heads turned to see the distiller's daughter, a twig in a rumpled chemise, trailing rope from her ankles and wrists as she flailed through the crowd.

"Papa," bawled Shifrah Puah amid universal imprecations against the evil eye, "she tied me up!"

Madame Treklekh, clattering jewelry and flapping jowls, bustled headlong to her daughter's side, as her husband rose puffing from his chair. "Rabbi ben Yedvab!" he bellowed, his whiskers repeating the scimitar curve of his pointed finger, "what is this?" The rebbe looked ruefully from Shifra Puah to her usurper, and frowned; then with a swiftness that belied his frailty, he again removed the bridal veil, silencing the crowd with the savage beauty he exposed.

"S-s-s-s-s," stammered the Saczer, until Velvl respectfully smote him between the shoulder blades. The old man caught his teeth in his hand, shoved them back into his mouth, and clicked them once to ascertain their working order. "Salka, sweetheart," he said tenderly, "you have to go back."

She'd assumed a defiant stance, arms folded over her breasts, shaking her head with a vehemence that dislodged the wig. Tresses tumbled from beneath it like unspooling yarn.

"*Hartseniu*," the rebbe was more sorrowful than threatening, a rare steadiness sustaining his speech, "don't make me have to lower the boom."

Visibly skittish, Salka sniffed and continued to stand her ground. Then liltingly for one so hoarse, the rebbe began to intone: "Return, return, O Shulammite, for love is strong as death, jealousy as cruel as the grave . . ."

Having expected some species of anti-demonic humbug, Hershel was puzzled to hear the rebbe reciting snatches from the Song of Songs—and these in a throaty rendition that sounded less like a conjuration than a lullabye. It was evident, though, from the set of her damson lips, the exaggerated lift of her chin, that the words were making the demoness ill at ease. Had her brazen masquerade somehow proven a miscalculation? In none of their tumultuous encounters had Hershel detected in Salka the least hint of vulnerability; and seeing it now, as she stood there defenseless before the gawking multitude, he was filled with conflicting emotions. Desperately he tried to displace his feelings with sober concerns: How-does-one-determine-the-kosherness-of-apples-grown-on-a-tree-in-a-yard-where-a-pig-was-slaughtered? How-assess-the-property-value-of-a-tower-floating-in-air? But it was no use. Once again he was enflamed with desire, only this time the fire in his loins, try as he might to douse it with reason, reached his heart.

"Who is she that looketh forth as the dawn," warbled the rebbe, "fair as the moon, fierce as an army with banners . . . ?"

Salka folded her arms more tightly, hugging herself.

Good, thought Hershel: whatever their sentiments, the *tzadik*'s words were having the proper effect; soon the creature, assaulted by righteousness, would be banished forever from their midst. Then he thought what he dimly recognized as sheer madness: I can save her.

"Salkeleh," the rebbe was personal again, stationary and unstuttering, "the boy isn't for you. This one's destined for a teacher."

"Then," she countered, the tremor in her voice betraying her agitation, "let first the teacher learn to be a man."

"He's not your type. In the flesh he ain't interested."

Hershel coughed and Salka, for all her extremity, managed the shadow of a smile. "A man who's too good for this world is no good for his bride."

"This one belongs to the Book," the Saczer insisted—and Hershel's head, swiveling back and forth between the *tzadik* and the daughter of Lilith, stopped at Rabbi ben Yedvab's ruined face. Never had it appeared so exalted, almost a young man's wearing the transparent mask of an old.

Then the creature spoke, so softly that she might have been inquiring of herself: "If he don't know from temptation, how will he know what to resist?"

His eyes having shifted back to her chastised radiance, Hershel could no longer contain himself. "I don't want to resist!" he cried, stretching his arms toward the object of his obsession. "Salka, I'm yours!" But instead of accepting his proffered embrace, she stiffened, confusion distorting her features, the last of her composure crumbling in the face of his need. It was as if, in disdaining the rebbe, Hershel had assumed *his* power over the creature, a daunting influence he had not sought. She shrank a step backward, her dark eyes aflicker with fear.

"Salka, don't worry, I'll save you!" declared Hershel, though he hadn't a clue as to what that might entail.

"Stay away from me!" she cautioned with outthrust hands.

" . . . Behold thou art fair," the rebbe had revived his chant, "thy navel like a rounded goblet, thy thighs the links of a golden chain . . . "

"But Salka," said Hershel, bewildered, "what are you saying? Aren't you . . . " he had first to swallow " . . . my wife?"

" . . . Thy teeth like a flock of ewes . . . "

"I'm nobody's wife, you *amhoretz*, you idiot! I'm a demon. All you did was break a spell, and that you didn't even do on purpose."

"But Salka, it's your Hershel! What are you afraid of?"

"It's you I'm afraid of."

"Salka, I love you!"

"Feh!" she spat, and was gone. She made a sudden reckless dash across the courtyard toward the tin-roofed study house, the guests parting before her like reeds.

Hershel turned back to the rebbe, who himself seemed abruptly deflated, requiring the aid of the faithful to raise his bony shoulders in a shrug. "It's love she c-c-c-can't stand," he said.

Suppressing an impulse to do the old man bodily harm, Hershel asked him, "How would you know?"

Again an assisted shrug. "Because I once loved her t-too." He explained that love had kept her trapped in the mirror, while desire brought her forth again. "But s-s-sometimes desire itself becomes sublime, and this the succubah-bahh [smack] the fiend cannot endure."

Aware of the intensity with which he was being regarded, Hershel stared back at the ogling assembly— at the row of would-be relations among whom the Treklekhs were trying to comfort their mortified daughter; at the poulterer and his wife who sat watching so complacently that they might have been enjoying a Purim shpiel. To them he felt oddly grateful: they were like some cozy couple who'd raised an imp the *sheydim* had substituted for their own lost child; and now the moment had come for the imp to return to his kind. Looking the rebbe full in his flinching face, Hershel reaffirmed the temptress's angry farewell: "Feh!" He shook off the groomsmen who tried to restrain him, picked up the skirts of his *kittl*, and flung himself after his bride.

Accompanied by students, disciples, and assorted wedding guests, Rabbi ben Yedvab entered the study house, finding it empty but for a petrified cat. He inspected the hall tree, then shakily (because he'd begun to twitch again), removed his talis, kissed it, and draped it over the mirror, as in a place where someone has died. No sooner had he done this, however, than the glass exploded in a hail of flying slivers and the prodigy crashed through the mirror from the other side. Tangled in the talis, Hershel plunged into the arms of the rebbe, who fell backward in turn into the open arms of his retinue.

Helped to his feet, the old *tzadik* (muttering a blessing over broken glass) sought to help a disoriented Hershel, pulling the blood-flecked cloth from his head. His lacerated face, framed by lank silver hair, was utterly strange, an arcane text his one-time rival Velvl Spfarb endeavored the rest of his days to construe. What he gleaned from the scholar's expression was the story he repeated years later, though nobody listened, in the shadow of the chimneys belching yellow smoke: how the bridegroom had discovered that *yenne velt*, the other side, was identical to this one, except that the ghosts there had more substance than the living. The echoes there were louder than their original noises, and the ancient history of the souls you encountered was more vivid than their current incarnations. Beauty there had a density of meaning that no scholar could penetrate—a terrible beauty that had stopped Hershel Khevreman in his tracks; and frightened of his own ignorance, having lost the object of his pursuit in the dusky distance, he'd turned around and beat a path back to the world. Only to find that the house of study and the town on the Carpathian heights were too desolate now to accomodate his longing. There was nothing left but to continue the chase, charging out the open door and following to its logical conclusion the route already taken by his heart.

THE NORTH OF GOD

"In his youth," said Velvl Spfarb, raising his voice to compete with the rattling of the cattle car and the caterwauling of its occupants, "the Talmud prodigy Hershel Khevreman fell in love with a lady demon. He chased her through a looking glass to Sitra Achra, the Other Side, where he lost her, and when he returned to this world, nothing was ever the same for him again . . . "

Velvl was keeping his promise to the young mother and her child, with whom he had been haphazardly thrown together in the crowd at the railyard, to tell them a story. Rather than exacted from the mother and daughter, however, it was a promise Velvl had made to himself. Meanwhile, all around him, the sealed car stuttered and groaned, its slats admitting slivers of sunlight that gashed the eyes. Supplications from a hundred mouths remained trapped beneath the ribs of the splintered ceiling, while the slop pails brimmed over, increasing the swill that lapped their ankles, the stench that stood better odds of reaching heaven than prayers.

"I suppose you could say," Velvl continued, "that Hershel Khevreman never really came all the way back to the world. His soul was no longer seated firmly in his body, and sometimes it tended to wander, which kept Hershel himself moving restlessly from village to village in its pursuit. A belch or a sneeze or, excuse me, a fortz might be enough to expel his soul, which in shape resembled a monkey with the face of a sad old man." This detail was for the child, whose eyes were plum bruises, her body (a plucked sparrow in a filthy smock) held suspended by her mother, with Velvl's help, above the muck at their feet. "A scholar of holy writ until his infatuation with the demoness Salka left him only half an inhabitant of the earth, Hershel sought work as a *melammed*, a teacher, in the towns he visited. But while he'd once committed whole tracts of Mishnah and Gemara to memory, his mind had contracted his soul's habit of wandering, and Hershel often found himself abandoning some hair-splitting point of law to entertain his unruly bochers with a story."

Unless you counted the dowdy Mehitabel, whom the bachelors in his market town of Stary Sacz would visit with the rabbi's dispensation, Velvl, despite his better than two score years, had never known a woman intimately. He felt a little ashamed that he should impose himself on this one, desolate in the absence of a husband who had doubtless perished in the current epidemic of death; but that his own death was also imminent (in light of God's refusal to make time stand still) emboldened him, and he'd resolved to try to beguile the young woman with a story of the legendary friend of his youth. Besides, pressed against her in the crush of human freight, with the child wedged awkwardly between them, it would have been more cruel to say nothing than to distract them with a frivolous tale.

"In the *shtetlach* where he relied on the hospitality of the townspeople, Hershel was perceived to be contaminating the children with his stories. There was the one about the mortifications inflicted upon his person by a saint to rid himself of an evil impulse; another about a daughter impregnated by her father's semen spilled in the *mikveh* where she bathed, and of the marvelous child subsequently born to her. I know these tales too," Velvl declared in the woman's ear, his temples beating with the boast, "but I will save them for another time."

Despite his lifelong bashfulness—a quality that seemed redundant in the jolting car, where every private function was exposed to public scrutiny—Velvl kept his eyes on the young mother, who, though she spoke not a word, kept her wary eyes fastened on him. Of course he hadn't counted on the amount of physical energy it would take to keep talking, so depleted was he by hunger and the stifling heat of their confinement; but her hollow face, half-hidden by a spill of oily umber hair, inspired him, and he realized there was no better reason to stay alive than to keep her spellbound. Her swatch of a daughter, who couldn't have been more than six, seemed to be listening just as attentively (though their fixed expressions might as easily have been attributed to fear), and while Velvl wondered at the appropriateness of his story for children, he decided that the circumstances lent all narratives equal appeal. In Gehenna, every story was a *bubbeh mayse*, a fairy tale.

He watched the mother (herself no more than a girl), gauging her expression for any signs of disapproval, as he told them that when Hershel wasn't run out of town for corrupting children, he had frequently to flee for his life from the husbands whose wives he defiled. Women, it seemed, were susceptible to his troubled countenance, his spaniel eyes and untended temple curls, and often, losing their heads, they offered their bodies as a means of mooring him to the world. For his part, seeking his vanished Salka in every maid and *balebosteh* he met, Hershel clove to each with a hornmad intensity. Like the pious cobbler Enoch who was translated to paradise as the archangel Metatron, he made love to them as if he were hammering the golden nail that spliced heaven to earth.

A woman wailed in lamentation or perhaps in the throes of childbirth; a rabbi and his disciple, both of them cowled in the upright shrouds of their prayer shawls, could be heard asking God to grant them the kiss of death; young people, reduced to their rawest instincts, ground themselves against one another in full view of the doleful company and, in their thirst, licked the sweat from each others' necks. If the press of bodies had enabled him to turn around, Velvl might have determined whether the drooping anatomy folded against his back were already deceased; he might have suffered the full impact of his situation and succumbed as well to his baser self. But the young widow's eyes—it was a safe bet that she was a widow—her coral eyes would not release him, nor would her daughter's, and while neither uttered a word, Velvl understood that he now had a mandate to continue the tale.

Still he expected that at any second the woman might snap out of her trance, clap hands over the little girl's ears, and cry, "*A shandeh*!" He ought to be ashamed of himself! But instead, Velvl discerned a fishtail flicker at the corner of her bloodless lips, which he decided was the stillbirth of a smile. He mourned its passing, then resolved that his story, which had veered from the meager facts he had about Hershel's life into a fable, half received and half invented, must never end. So long as he could keep the mother and daughter captivated, he could keep them safe.

"Sometimes Hershel would hire himself out as a scribe, writing letters for illiterate matzoh-bakers and sinew-pluckers to their relations in America, or letters of blackmail to delinquent husbands from their deserted wives. He also wrote letters to dead ancestors from families asking them to intervene on their behalf in paradise, and occasionally he would dispatch missives from the ancestors themselves in response to the requests from their families. These also resulted in his being chased out of town by irate rabbis and their duped congregations; and while experience had made Hershel relatively fast on his feet, his flight was often hampered by the wives who wished to accompany him and the children who clung to his gangly legs . . . "

At this point the young mother, leaving Velvl to support her pendant daughter—he was profoundly grateful for the trust—freed a hand to dredge the pocket of her torn pinafore, removing a stiff crust of black bread which she offered the child. But while the child contemplated the bread as if she'd forgotten what food was for, it was snatched from the widow's hand by a spidery neighbor, pince-nez riding his needle nose like a capsized bicycle. Stuffing his mouth so that the bread filled his concave cheeks, he chomped ferociously, his otherwise expressionless face inches away from the mother and child.

He was wandering the roads, Hershel Khevreman, in the Carpathian foothills above the plague-stricken town of Zshldzh on a perfect morning in early May, when he felt the call of nature. He left the wagon-rutted highway, crossed the railroad tracks, and ducked into a locust grove, where he heard voices from a glade in the distance. Always on the lookout for soldiers that might try to conscript him into the army of the Czar, from which Jewish lads seldom returned, he instinctively hid himself behind a tree. But prompted by the curiosity that had dogged him throughout his travels, he left his rucksack on the ground to creep closer and saw that the voices did in fact belong to a pair of soldiers, their untethered horses cropping clover nearby. They were members of a Cossack brigade from the look of them, who had cast off their military tunics, which lay draped over a juniper bush, and stood facing each other across a clearing afloat with dandelions, each of them holding a raised service revolver in his hand. Hershel had always understood that such encounters were conducted with ritual formality, with doctors and seconds standing by to conduct the protocol. But here the older of the two soldiers, dressed like the younger in overblouse and calfskin boots, a gold ring aglint in his ear, orchestrated the moment. "Fire," he pronounced, in so even a voice that Hershel, who understood Russian, half expected him to name the other three elements as well. Then, without hesitating, the elder Cossack lowered his pistol and fired a shot through the porcelain forehead of the younger before that one had even leveled his piece.

Hershel's heart knocked at his ribcage like a fist at a door, as he watched the man holster his still-smoldering revolver, then pivot on his heel to don the smart officer's tunic. He gathered up the reins of the dead man's horse even as he mounted his own and, spurring his beast's velvet flank, cantered off without a backward glance, leaving his vanquished foe lying face-up in a bed of nettles. Still incapable of motion, Hershel looked on from behind a shrub at the lifeless youth, wondering what events could have dictated his premature death on this tranquil spring morning. Perhaps the officer had a young bride who'd looked fondly on the recruit, who, innocent of her regard, had nonetheless received from her husband a challenge his honor would not let him refuse. Maybe the absence of witnesses was due to the impropriety of an officer's dueling with an enlisted man. In the midst of his speculations Hershel saw a honeybee spiral downward and alight on the soldier's brow as if to sip the nectar of his blood. The first bee was soon joined by a second and a third, until a buzzing swarm had assembled to obscure the youth's beardless face, which resembled a sunflower from which all petals had been plucked. Compelled by a sympathetic impulse, Hershel left his blind and darted into the clearing to shoo away the bees. But before he could reach the fallen Cossack, the swarm, ascending in corkscrew formation, took flight of its own accord. In their wake, the soldier's handsome face had aged, his formerly prominent jaw having receded into a stringy yellow beard, his eyes—red-rimmed and rheumy— open now and staring at Hershel, who froze again in his tracks. Then the youth's wizened replacement stirred and began with an *oy* to raise himself to his feet, his joints crackling from the effort, the belted blouse and riding breeches hanging on his bony frame like loose skin. To the rigid Hershel Khevreman he remarked,

"These gentile *shmattes*, they don't never fit good."

Frightened out of his paralysis, Hershel backed up a few steps, about-faced, and took off at a sprint. He forgot his rucksack and, having failed to empty his bladder, shamed himself in his headlong flight toward he knew not where. Ever since his exile from the yeshiva in Stary Sacz after his affair with the wanton Salka, he'd been wandering aimlessly. The girl, whose notoriety once prompted the local rabbi to brand her a "daughter of Lilith," had enticed him away from his precious books; then fleeing the ensuing scandal herself, she had seemed to vanish from the face of the earth. She left behind her, in place of the celebrated scholar (patronized by rich merchants and fought over by rival matchmakers), a disgraced and heartbroken pariah, his studious nature supplanted by fancies beyond his control. From that moment Hershel was possessed of an unrelenting restlessness that hounded him from town to town. All who knew him said he was looking for the absconded girl, but whenever he reached a place where his reputation had not preceded him, he tried to establish himself as a member in good standing of the community. Eventually, however, he would succumb again to an unrighteous urge. Grown bored with instructing unruly boys in their *alef-bais*, for instance, Hershel might reclaim their attention by telling them some indecorous story from a forbidden book. The boys would carry the tales home to their fathers, who fumed, while their mothers, at the risk of appearing unseemly, would pause at the windows of the *bet hamidrash* to eavesdrop. Occasionally one became so enraptured that she would steal into the study house at night, where she would slide next to Hershel on his pallet behind the woodstove and offer to swap certain favors for another of his exotic tales. Exposed in the end for his iniquity, the hedge teacher would be sent packing, abandoning the ruined wife and the town on the run as he fled in search of another temporary home.

Along the highways he was inclined to drink a bit. He stopped at taverns where even the local peasants would stand him a schnapps in exchange for his stories, which he could de-Judaize on demand, substituting for the *sheydim* and *kapelyushniklim*, the unclean spirits of his standard fare, Polish demons and Baba Yagas by the score. Sometimes in his cups, Hershel was subject to hallucinations, fantastic affairs that trumped the quotidian, and once in a while the visions came over him without the agency of alcohol. Afterwards he would feel listless and empty, as if his very soul had taken leave of his breast, not in itself an unpleasant sensation. But in time the impulse to be filled again by some moonlit glimpse of an alternate existence would reassert itself, and he would long for the intensity of his visions. When the intensity overcame him again, however, unnerved by its power, Hershel would pray for the dullness to return. Give him the ordinary world, which knew its own limits and followed strict laws forbidding incursions of the impossible. But the familiarity of the ordinary world invariably bred contempt, and Hershel would ache all over again for transcendence. It was a condition that made him feel that he lived in neither one world nor the other, and as a consequence he had known no peace since his yeshiva days.

Still reeling from the spectacle of the old yid resurrected from a dead Russian youth, Hershel told himself that it was nothing, the kind of illusion normal men were prone to as a result of, say, a fever.

That was it: he had experienced the first effects of a typhus delirium, having contracted the disease during his ill-advised transit through Zshldzh. The thought alone was enough to bring on a rash succeeded by an enfeebling nausea. Having run beyond his lungs' capacity to sustain him or his legs' to hold him erect, Hershel staggered to the side of the road, where he vomited into a shallow ditch. This was no perfunctory upchucking, however: his body heaved in a seismic convulsion that seemed to turn him inside-out. Bits of fat and potato from the Shabbos cholent a family had given him only that morning spewed lava-like out of his mouth. It was a mighty ejaculation that triggered a riposte in his nether parts, and so rocked was Hershel from the shock of it that, when it subsided, he pitched head foremost into the ditch.

This was his situation when he was discovered by a passing crone. She had the appearance of an old speaker woman of the type that sold talismans outside the bathhouse and delivered and aborted babies with equal insouciance. While her frame was gaunt, her hips were broad from the half-dozen or so peasant skirts she wore despite the vernal season, and she carried a bundle of kindling in a hamper strapped to her back. Spying Hershel, she continued on to her hovel, then returned with a wooden barrow into which, robust for her years, she loaded the inert young man.

"He came to his senses on a flock-stuffed mattress in a dwelling that seemed little more than a sty with a damp turf roof, opening his eyes on a kerchiefed creature whose ugliness inspired a measure of awe. The flesh of her face was pitted and embossed as if a starfish had been plastered across it, her chin whiskers like the spines of a prickly pear. She was leaning over him in order to scrub his soiled behind with a sponge, the spicy simoom of her breath (in odd contrast to her loathsome features) vying with the stink of his parts. When she had completed her ministrations, allowing him to roll onto his back, she dropped the sour sponge into a bucket and brought to his lips a clay cup whose bouquet revived the pungency she had just dispelled. Squinching his nostrils against the fumes, Hershel brushed her arm aside. This was more an involuntary reflex than a reaction to stench and monstrosity, since, having voided his soul along with his breakfast, Hershel tended to view the beautiful and grotesque with the same dispassion. But when the old woman set aside the cup and began to unbutton the bodice of her weskit, Hershel experienced a squeamishness that overcame his torpor. She had slipped out of her haircloth dirndl (and the calico and the duck cloth skirts under that), unpeeling the layers of herself like an onion until she stood before him clad only in a gray muslin shift. But before she could remove the shift with its unraveling ruffle and slip into the bed beside him, revealing a body he imagined was covered in scales, Hershel sat bolt upright and, despite his recent debilitation, gathered the scant sheet about his loins, sprang from the bed, and made a precipitous dash through the doorway of her hut."

Here Velvl paused in his description of Hershel's

flight to draw a breath, which he released in a plangent sigh. His audience—was she still his audience? for the woman's frayed lids had grown heavier, hooding her eyes—his audience was reduced now to one, since the child had fallen asleep. It was good she could sleep in spite of the jostling car's mounting cacophony, but in slumber her slight bones were leaden, and Velvl struggled along with the widow to keep the child (who slumped like a ragdoll) from sliding into the stew in which they stood. Periodically the transport would sound its whistle, which might have passed for the reedy whine of an ordinary train, though this one contained passengers bound for no earthly destination. A trickle of lumpy brown broth coated Velvl's arm, signaling that the girl had also succumbed to the dysentery that was rife in the railway car. He stiffened from a nausea that gripped his vitals, which were pasted like (he pictured) wet cellophane against the internal wall of his spine. This fascinated Velvl, his emaciation, since he'd been plump as a capon all his days, but while he told himself that travail had reconstituted him into the leanness of a man of action, in his mind Velvl Spfarb was still soft and round—and there was no world, even one with a future, in which he would ever have had the chance to make a home with this woman and her child.

Blades of light impaled the interior of the car like swords through a magician's box, turning red as if freshly forged before growing dim; but instead of taking up again where he'd left off, the storyteller hesitated, submitting to the widow tentatively, "Ich heyst, my name . . . is Velvl." Did he really think that, from the depths of their shared degradation, she would fetch a response? "I'm Manya or Rokhl or Ruth," he imagined her saying. "I was born in ——sk, where my mother read us the novels of Abraham Mapu and feather-stitched the borders of our drawers, and our Papa, an installment peddler, brought back from his travels in Kiev and Dnepropretrovsk treasures that for our dowries he would sock away . . . " But of course she remained silent, and as for her face, Velvl was unable to see it now with much clarity. Since losing his spectacles in the mayhem at the Kazimierz railyard, he perceived everything through a grainy fog that dulled the edges of a universe he was anyway tired of looking at. Besides, it was growing dark, the widow swaying before him in graceful silhouette.

An unthinkable notion occurred to Velvl: without the cataclysm that had befallen the Jews, estranging them from hope, he would never have had (*dayenu*) even this small portion of family. He would have continued in his solitary vocation as Reb Grynszpan's humble assistant in his general merchandise on the market platz. There, a competent if uninspired salesclerk in a sailcloth apron pulled over his talis koton, he sold bulk flour and lentils to zloty-pinching Jews and goyim alike; he took scrupulous inventory of horsetack and goosedown and spirit lamps, and attended as in a sleepwalk the patch-roofed synagogue, the study house, and the ritual bath. He would have continued renting his drafty quarters in Madam Binstock's annex, shoring up holes with the pages of holy books, listening at night to the creaking bedstead above him as his landlady entertained Berish the butcher and his leonine groans. He would have carried on making his lonely Shabbos every Friday night, and afterward visiting Mehitabel, for whom he stood in a queue of guilty bachelors as if outside a *mikveh*. Upon his turn in her puncheon-floored kennel, she would cast off the tatty gown she needn't have bothered putting on in the first place, exhibiting skin so slack it resembled another sallow garment. She would invite him, after the receipt of a few kopeks, to embrace the folds of her ample flesh, inserting him into what may have been an orifice or perhaps just another fold.

Then a Russian regiment entered Stary Sacz and erected a statue of Lenin, only to retreat before the advance of the Germans, who forced the Jews to bury the statue with full orthodox honors. At first the *shtetl* thought, just another pogrom—hadn't they already endured the worst the century had to offer? But this time the Jews that weren't shot outright, or hanged or flayed or burned alive in the torched synagogue, were rounded up and deported to the city of Cracow. In the slough of the Kazimierz ghetto, its walls constructed in the shape of Jewish tombstones, Velvl's intestines were coiled like an armature around a living lump of fear, which was nothing new: fear had fueled him since his yeshiva days. Fear of poverty, of cholera, gentiles, women, fear of his own weak-chinned face in a mirror—the list had no end. But here in a place dedicated to the manufacture of fear—a place that one ghoul of a rebbe declared was located to the north of God, where His jurisdiction no longer held sway—

Velvl found himself developing a certain resistance.

Not that he partook of the ingenuity of the doomed, who bartered, bribed, and smuggled, printed newspapers, played sonatas, danced macabre fox-trots and told tasteless jokes in impromptu cellar cabarets, even as they starved; they hauled the hayricks of corpses with tricycle-propelled hearses, brewed poppyseed decoctions to make children forget their hunger, and wrote acerbic suicide notes. Some even threaded the labyrinth of sewers beneath the streets, emerging in cemeteries at the edge of the city whence they fled to the forests to join the partisans—or so went the rumors to which Velvl never quite subscribed. Though he knew now that nothing was true, that all was permitted, he persisted in sleepwalking toward his own quietus, feeling he had a headstart on his coreligionists. Sometimes he even felt that he had outwitted death, having already crossed over, while his limbs still went reflexively through the motions of survival. Every day he put on the heavy greatcoat with its jaundiced star, presented himself for the dawn shape-up, and marched out the ghetto gates through the city to the brickyard six kilometers away. There, for want of a horse, he and several others towed the bar like blind Samsons round and round the stone mixer that turned the treadles that mixed the clay. He slogged back again in a burnt orange twilight with frostbitten cheeks, the muscles of his heart enflamed, to his reward of ten ounces of stale bread and tepid water bobbing with potato peels. He made his way through unending funeral processions, past the galleries of figures with pipe-cleaner bodies and heads like extinguished bulbs, peddling bones boiled in urine, gold fillings, half-forgotten lullabyes, themselves. In a house with no roof he flopped on a lice-seething mattress under stairs that murmured and drummed like the erratic heartbeat of a wooden beast, but while he experienced a fatigue beyond exhaustion, sleep wouldn't come.

He lay tugging idly at his hair and beard, which came out in gorse-like clumps, feeling the calluses forming on his brain as they had on his hands. Thoughts never vexed him; thoughts were too fettered to free themselves from stupor, let alone gain the altitude of dreams—not that dreaming was a faculty Velvl had any aptitude for. Nearly impervious to his fate, he was nevertheless interested to discover that, at the end of the day, he was still alive and that he seemed to take a measure of pride in the fact. In the small hours he might feel the ping of a memory against his brainpan, and while he had neither the energy nor desire to invite it in, the memory, like a percolating vapor, would eventually trickle through. Then enter Hershel Khevreman, the longlost friend whose heretical behavior had once scandalized a whole town. In truth they were never really close, Velvl and Hershel; and if Velvl were honest, he would have had to admit that he recalled the scholar with a touch of envy, not to say resentment, for the effortlessness with which Hershel had acquired the learning that Velvl, Hershel's only real competitor, had once strived so hard to attain.

Both boys had had a passion for the legal aspect of Talmud at the expense of its more desultory narrative dimension. But Hershel had betrayed his calling, and Velvl, along with the others, condemned him as a free-thinker and *meshumed*, an apostate. So why was it that now, when the whole earth had surrendered to death's dominion, Velvl should suddenly conceive the habit of remembering Hershel's fabled sins?

Shifting his grip on the little girl, an operation that cost him no end of pain in his kishkes and spine, Velvl went on with his story: "Padding down the highway in his stockinged feet, the sheet wrapped about his naked body toga-style, Hershel passed the crossroads where he'd spat up his gorge, overtaking a bandy-legged old man. It was the same old man, he realized, that he'd encountered earlier that day in the glade, though this one had exchanged his ill-fitting military garb for a familiar mufti . . . "

Having already trotted beyond the old man, Hershel came to a halt, turning around to say aloud to himself, "He's wearing my clothes." For a brief moment Hershel entertained the random fancy that the old man might be his own aged self, then dismissed the notion as an aftershock of his temporary illness. He noted too that the geezer was carrying his weathered rucksack.

"Nu," croaked the old man, approaching Hershel with perfect assurance as he responded to the young man's overheard accusation, "I don't know what you're talking, but you should understand I'm a generous type. Maybe you will find in here something for yourself?" Saying which, he offered the rucksack to Hershel, who snarled as he tore it from the old man's hands and, self-conscious at wearing only a bedsheet in the middle of the Czar's highway, dove into the bag foraging for clothes. What he found was a saffron blouse and some striped riding breeches, plus a pair of folded leather boots. With a vague sense of having seen them before, Hershel wondered why he should don a stranger's apparel when his own hung on the back of this simpering old specimen? Well, for one thing, his own clothes were beggarly, the caftan having lost the nap of its squirrel fur collar, the whole ensemble no doubt befouled by its contact with the thief. On the other hand, you had to question the wisdom of a Jew wearing a Cossack's attire. But as he tried on the high-collared overblouse experimentally, and stepped into the snug breeches, Hershel thought the outfit rather becoming, and the knee-high boots were a great improvement over the practically soleless bast shoes the fellow had also appropriated. Moreover, with regard to his own clothes, Hershel thought he would rather burn them than wear them again after their violation by this fleabitten kucker.

Further inspecting the canvas bag for the remainder of his belongings, Hershel found, along with his neglected phylacteries and prayer shawl and his limp edition of Judah Halevi's poems, a miscellany of unusual items. They included a rope, a hinged stick resembling a serpent's forked tongue, and an ivory-handled revolver. Seeing the gun awakened in Hershel's mind, still fuzzy from fever, the memory of the duel and the unaccountable materialization of the crookbacked old man. Chilled to the marrow, he withdrew the gun from the bag, holding its handle as he might have the tail of a rat. The old man raised his hands.

"Don't shoot!"

"I'm not going to shoot you," said Hershel, wanting only to make short work of this encounter. "You can put your hands down."

"Don't shoot!" reiterated the old man.

Said Hershel, "Are you deaf? I'm not going to shoot you." Though he wasn't quite sure how he ought to dispose of the weapon.

Then, without lowering his arms, the old man modulated his voice to an undertone, as if someone might be listening. "Pretend you're holding me up."

Hershel was incredulous. "What?"

"A favor, Comrade Cossack, if you please," the old man whispered. "Pretend you're a *ganef*, you're holding me up."

"But I'm neither a robber nor a Cossack," insisted Hershel.

"I said *pretend*," barked the old man, then reverted to his solicitous tone. "The items in that bag, they don't belong to me, and the people they belong to will never believe I was robbed."

Hershel stared a moment at the old man through narrowed eyes, then shrugged: whatever his mysterious origin, he was clearly a lunatic. But so relieved was Hershel to be clothed again, to have escaped so handily his brush with illness and worse, that he had half a mind to humor this curiosity. "So what can *I* do about it?" he inquired in the spirit of the charade, tightening his hold on the handle of the gun.

"Allow me to hang on a fencepost my cap that you can shoot in it some holes, so I got proof I was robbed." Then, before Hershel could digest his logic, or lack of same, the old man had scuttled across a shallow defile and draped the peaked cap (which also belonged to Hershel and was already porous) over a knotty fencepost. Looking both ways to make certain they weren't being observed, Hershel waved the old man away from the fence, and though he'd never fired a gun in his life, gripped the weapon with both hands, took aim, and pulled the trigger. The report jarred his frame, which vibrated like a struck tuning fork, and flushed some birds from a nearby copse, but when the smoke cleared, the cap was still unscathed. As thrilled as he was shaken by his action, Hershel sighted his target now with a single eye, then fired the pistol again and yet again, until one of the bullets, finally striking its mark, blew the cap from the post. The old man congratulated him on his marksmanship, eliciting from Hershel a foolish grin, then removed the gaberdine caftan and draped it over the fencepost, requesting that Hershel perforate this garment as well. Trigger-happy now, Hershel was only too willing to oblige, but this time the weapon, emptied of rounds, responded with only a click.

"Sorry," he said, himself disappointed, "no more holes."

The old man showed the jagged stumps of his teeth. "That's all I wanted to know," he said, and straightaway leaped upon Hershel, knocking him to the ground. Preternaturally strong for his years, he managed in an instant to pin the younger man to the patchy earth, pincering his wrists with a single talon-like hand, while with the other he reached into the open rucksack for the rope. When he'd finished trussing the length and breadth of the counterfeit Cossack, who cursed him violently as he struggled against his restraints, the old man got back to his feet and, panting only slightly, instructed his victim, "Now you say: 'That proves it, you can't trust a Jew!'"

Squirming to no effect, Hershel continued to threaten and curse ("May your enemies get cramps from dancing on your grave!"), but the old man refused to release him until he repeated the punchline.

"Okay," muttered Hershel grudgingly. "That proves it, you can't trust a Jew." "Once more with feeling," enjoined the old man.

Hershel sighed and repeated the line, prompting the old man to whack him over the head with the spring-hinged stick he'd removed from the bag, its slap resounding like another pistol report. Then he stooped to untie his hostage, declaring, "Tahkeh, you got a natural gift for theater!"

Dusting himself off as he rose, Hershel growled, "Meshugeh ahf toit!", and short of strangling the old loon with his bare hands (a dicey proposition given the fellow's fortitude), spat against the evil eye and abruptly began to walk away. Before he'd advanced many steps down the road, however, the old man called out to him, "Pardon, Comrade Cossack, but may I ask where is it you think you are going?"'

Anxious as he was to distance himself from the maniac, Hershel couldn't help but marvel at the man's presumption. Returning arrogance for arrogance, he swiveled around to tell the old party, "I'm going in search of my immortal soul." Then it surprised him to find that he felt all at once like a character out of one of his own stories.

"Ah," said the old man, wistfully, "that I can't help you with. But if it's for gainful employment you are looking, which from your lack of resources you seem in need of, I might be able to offer some assistance. Allow me to introduce myself: Elihu Hanover, impresario and director of the Pishtipl Players Touring Company, at your service, and always I am on the lookout for new talent. Having canvassed the towns in this region for suitable venues, I am currently en route to rendezvous with my people in Drogobych, and since you are already in costume, so to speak, and got an obvious thespian flare, I invite you to accompany me."

Indignant, Hershel replied, "I'm no *shauspieler*!", but before he could turn his back on the man a second time, his temper had cooled enough that he began to think better of what he had said. After all, since departing the yeshiva eons ago, swapping halakhic strictures for eccentric tales, what else would you call what he'd done but performance? Besides, having no destination of his own, why shouldn't he attach himself to another's, and who knew but this screwball might be amusing company? He might, for instance, be a cure for the melancholy that was an apparently lingering symptom of his recent disease. So, after another shrug and a hastily shared Shehechayanu, the two itinerants set off down the road together, leaving behind them a smoking pistol in the weeds.

Said Velvl, speaking to the widow as Hershel: "'I'm going in search of my immortal soul.'"

"'Ah,' said the old man, supremely confident, 'that I can help you with.' Then he introduced himself as Elihu Hanovi, the prophet Elijah the Tishbite, incarnate for a spell during one of his earthly visitations.

"'Of course you are,' said Hershel, perfectly aware of the cycle of legends about the prophet Elijah, who had ascended to heaven alive in a flaming chariot but returned to earth in various guises to intervene on behalf of the oppressed. Hadn't he recounted for his pupils numerous, often perverse variations of the stories himself? Naturally Hershel understood that the poor soul before him was completely mad, but still suffering some lingering symptoms of melancholy from his recent illness, he thought it might be amusing to have him as company along the way. So, with a shrug and a common Shehechayanu, the two of them fell into step with one another."

Around dusk of their first night together, Hershel and Reb Hanover entered the village of Zitsk on the Lower Bug, where they appealed at the half-door of an inn for a handout. The innkeeper's daughter, a cow-eyed lump of a girl, told them that, alas, there was nothing in the house to eat, or at least that's what her father, the innkeeper, who was away on a provisioning trip, had instructed her to inform any vagabond schnorrers. Hershel tugged at Reb Hanover's sleeve and signaled with his chin toward a freshly flicked chicken lying on the kitchen cutting board.

"A pity," said Reb Hanover to the girl, after a not-so-furtive wink at Hershel. "But didn't your father tell you also that any passing stranger could be possibly the prophet Elijah, and that he might be carrying with him his magic staff?" He presented the gnarled walking stick he'd broken from a hickory branch earlier that day. "With this staff," he declared, "I can cook a meal fit for Messiah. I have only to stir it in a pot of boiling water."

The girl's bovine eyes grew wider, her lantern jaw working speechlessly, as she admitted the two travelers into the pewter-hung kitchen. She put a large pot of water on the castiron stove, and while they waited for the pot to boil, Reb Hanover breezily shmoozed the credulous girl; while Hershel, as was his habit whenever he was under a roof, breathed deeply the warmth of the domestic atmosphere. When the steam rose, the old man began to stir the pot with his stick, asking the girl, "You don't have by chance a marrowbone, and maybe some chicken giblets, and a little kosher salt?"

"What a question," said the girl, scurrying in her shapeless wrapper to fetch a bone, giblets, and salt from the larder. Bidding her dump them in the pot, Reb Hanover continued to stir, asking after a moment for a pareve carrot, if you please, and some cabbage and groats. The girl produced them all, adding on her own initiative a turnip and onions, while Reb Hanover kept stirring until a fragrant aroma filled the low-ceilinged room. When the girl had finished setting the swayback table, the old man made a blessing and ladled them each a hearty bowlful of soup from the pot.

Tasting it with a wooden spoon, the girl licked her meaty lips and began to extol the virtues of the magic stick. "Perhaps," she inquired, albeit haltingly, "you would like to sell it?"

"Heaven forbid!" exclaimed Reb Hanover. "The staff is my inheritance, a gift from the angel Raziel himself, a hairloom of the arch-seraphim. And yet, hmm, you're such a fine young woman, and with such a generous heart . . ."

"What would you take for it?" The girl's eagerness was betrayed by the pumpkin flush of her cheeks. "A ruble?"

Reb Hanover frowned, and wagged his grizzled head, "I couldn't accept for it no money."

"Then what would you take?"

"No money, that's final. The staff is much too sacred that in a profane transaction I should exchange it." Then becoming thoughtful: "But if you give me that freshly killed chicken," indicating the cutting board, "and throw in perhaps a ruble for good measure, I'll make for you a present of the illustrious thing."

With the fat hen, plus the condiments and bottle of schnapps the ruble bought, Reb Hanover and Hershel were able to provide a feast for themselves, which they shared with the luftmenschen hunkered about the stove in the paupers' study house. The next morning, when they departed the village, Reb Hanover asked Hershel Khevreman, who was becoming more impressed with his companion by the hour, "Can you write?"

"Some say like an angel," Hershel admitted.

"Then write up for some stage business the story what we just done."

Hershel wondered since when was he taking orders from the geezer, then remembered that he was technically in Reb Hanover's employ, and besides, he thought he might be able to do something interesting with the story.

"And that," said Velvl, jammed so close to the widow that his lips brushed the moist down of her cheek, "was the beginning of the star-crossed collaboration between Hershel Khevreman and the prophet Elijah." He and the woman had managed to settle the little girl in the puddle of her bones atop a battered suitcase bound with twine, above which Velvl and her mother were shoved helplessly against one another. The vault that their bodies formed above the child assumed some of the load their legs could now scarcely support, but their convergence bore more resemblance to a wrestling hold than an embrace. Nevertheless, the forced contact intensified the plummeting sensation in his gut that Velvl identified as a symptom of love.

Somewhere close by, the rabbi, disappointed at having been denied God's personal coup de grâce, droned in the holy tongue to his disciple: "70,000 heads has each scorpion of the Reich, and each sting 70,000 vesicles filled with poison which we sinners are compelled to drink. Our eyes melt in their sockets from the fear of scorpions . . . " No other individual voices could be heard. The crescendo having come and gone, the noise in the car was subdued to soft weeping and the burbling of those who were drowning in the blood from their own ruptured hearts. Occasionally a candle might flare—though who had the resources to light a candle? The light would reveal a swell of rag-swaddled limbs cresting into a wave, poised to crash against the sides of the cattle car. Then the condensation of filth that had climbed the walls of the car to rain in a perpetual drizzle from the ceiling would snuff the candle out.

Velvl had no more illusions. Unlike during his early days in the ghetto, he was not deceived; he knew he wasn't dead yet, that this was still a man-made hell, though after this what surprises could God's black eternity have to offer? There was of course the old canard of deliverance, of peace in the hereafter, but while the impulse to survive had never been strong in Velvl, crossing over now seemed an almost gratuitous step. What was more, since encountering the widow, he'd become possessed of the notion, perhaps depraved, that even this monstrous journey qualified as an adventure; it was a corollary to the kind of narrative in which, for instance, the prophet Elijah, while promising to reunite a young man with his derelict soul, leads him on a reckless ramble down a crooked path. How was it possible, though, that in all this hurt a story, any story, could still prick his heart (a bladder too parched and deflated even to burst) with a splinter of light? But the splinter had to be drawn out before the wound turned septic; it must be milled on the lathe of the tale that Velvl was spinning for the woman, whose body spasmed with hiccupping sobs in his arms. Could he finish the story, he wondered, before the train reached its destination? Did he even know how the story ended? But the conclusion was not so important as keeping his audience a willing captive, thereby protecting her from an awareness of the greater captivity. The task lent Velvl an ardor far beyond his modest means, and he believed that, so long as he continued to tell Hershel's story—even now as the train began to slow down—he was himself a sanctuary for the wandering scholar's fugitive soul.

Said Velvl into the whorls of the widow's ear: "It was not a good time to be abroad in the land, though when was it ever a good time for a Jew to be abroad in the land? There were mounted hussars, secret police, marauding bandits, smoldering villages laid waste by peasants who blamed the Jews for their oppression, villages deserted after wholesale evictions. There was a failed revolution. In a city to the north, advised by evil councilors, the Czar had some poor zhlub hauled up on trial for ritual murder, while the Czar's wife romped with a fiendish monk and the Order of the Black Hundreds fomented universal pogroms. Leery of such goings-on, Hershel and his companion took the roads that kept mainly to the outskirts of history. During their travels Elijah cured toothaches and caused a man who had swallowed a reptile to cough it back up again, but he was as likely to play pranks on those he deemed deserving of retribution as to perform good works. These were childish pranks, often involving, forgive me, the animal functions with which the prophet seemed mildly obsessed, complaining that, no matter how youthful the body he inhabited, it turned old once his soul was in residence—old and incontinent. He was known to sprinkle coins over a bowlful of drek and invite the unsuspecting to grab a handful; he peddled his own pebbly turds in the marketplace as 'prophet's berries,' which, ingested, were guaranteed to bring visions of Messiah. In an inn, where they'd connived a room in exchange for some magic tricks, Elijah shat in Hershel's bed and laughed himself sick when Hershel, whom the prophet alleged was in need of chronic abasement, received the blame. Once he blessed a poor man, assuring him that the first thing he undertook would have no end until the man himself cried, 'Enough!' When the man started to tally up his few meager kopeks, they multiplied in profusion until he lost count. Then a greedy couple, having gotten wind of the prophet's benefice, applied to Elijah for a similar blessing. 'May the first thing you do have no end,' said Elijah, after which the wife said to her husband, 'That we may count gold upon gold undisturbed, let us first attend to our most urgent physical needs.' So they did—and they had to continue until their lives were extinct. Another time, along the road, Elijah wrestled the Angel of Death, who had challenged him in the guise of a kulak disrespectful of his age, and the prophet would have defeated him had not God intervened to save the Angel's neck; for death must retain its hegemony in the affairs of men.

"While he was often bewildered by Elijah's protean devices, Hershel remained intrigued, and found himself not only unable to quit the old man but also compelled to chronicle his often irrational actions. That he was himself periodically the butt of those actions did not discourage him—it was apparently the price of the prophet's company, and Hershel was convinced that Elijah would ultimately lead him back to what he had lost."

Crossing a bridge over a millrace on the road to Drogobych, Reb Hanover lifted a leg to let fly a resonant fart.

Remarked Hershel, "It seems, sir, that you suffer from wind."

Reb Hanover: "What do you mean, suffer?" withdrawing his hinged paddle from its sheath to whack Hershel over the head. Hershel winced, though he was growing accustomed to the occasional drubbing: it was apparently the price of the old man's company. How strange that he was so willing to pay the price. Then Reb Hanover said, "You be the Cossack and I'll be the Jew." It had become a routine injunction, though Hershel's apparel, a liability in any case, had lately grown too shabby to identify as military garb. "Now say to me, 'What makes you Jews so smart?'"

Hershel had half a mind to suggest that the old man be the Cossack for a change, but dutiful straight man (not to say recording secretary) that he was, he repeated, "Tahkeh, what makes you Jews so smart?"

"It'sh becaush we eat the headsh of whitefish," replied Reb Hanover, having stuffed his mouth with a piece of dried sturgeon. "Now shay," swallowing the bolus in his throat and licking his fingers clean, "'If that's the secret, then I can be as smart as you.'"

Hershel repeated the line.

"That's right," said Reb Hanover, "and in fact I happen to have an extra whitefish head with me. You can have it for five kopeks." Stepping briefly out of character: "Now you give to me the five kopeks."

"I don't have five kopeks."

"Pretend."

Hershel pretended to fork over the currency.

"Right. Now I tell the audience that he goes away, the Cossack, and comes back in an hour. 'Listen, Jew,' says the Cossack," nodding to Hershel, who repeated, "Listen, Jew . . ." "'. . . you sold me that whitefish head for five kopeks, but I just saw in the market a whole whitefish for only three.' Now you say it."

Hershel: "You sold me that whitefish head, et cetera . . ."

"See," replied Reb Hanover smugly, "you're getting smarter already!" And again he whacked Hershel with his paddle, prompting Hershel to take out his notepad and jot down the dialogue.

By the time they reached the town of Drogobych

in southern Galicia, its rooftops spread like a crazyquilt over a lumpy mattress, Hershel had already added several new pieces to the Pishtipl repertoire. Elihu Hanover's acquaintance, it seemed, had lit a fire under him. On their arrival, he was introduced to the company as both shpieler and author, his credentials accepted at face value since the motley theatrical troupe had never had a resident playwright before. All their productions had previously consisted of cobbled improvisations and plays freely adapted from standard Yiddish fare. They had been quartered in Moshe Baumgarten's galleried inn, the Pishtipls, whose cramped sleeping chambers and saloon they'd overrun to the exclusion of further guests. They'd consumed tubs of kreplach and barrels of Muscat wine, bestrewing the premises with a blizzard of unpaid bills. The innkeeper's irate appeals to the authorities for their ouster, however, had fallen upon deaf ears, since the local constabulary had already been suborned by the attentions of wayward soubrettes, who had effectively turned the inn into a brothel. As a consequence, Reb Baumgarten greeted the returning impresario in a fit of pique. To appease the angry innkeeper, whose beard appeared to curl and extend with his every outburst, the impresario assured him he would be amply compensated just as soon as the troupe mounted their new Purim shpiel. This was an original production, conceived and created by the celebrated dramaturge Hershel Khevreman.

"Purim!" protested Moshe Baumgarten, the tip of whose beard tickled Reb Hanover's nostrils. "It ain't even Shavuos yet." To which Reb Hanover, after sneezing, proudly proclaimed,

"It's always Purim when the Pishtipls come to town."

Hershel's play, performed in a flagstone courtyard between the *bet hamidrash* and a blistered tannery wall, combined elements of political satire with his own trademark habit of longing. It also included selected episodes inspired by his travels with Reb Hanover. Mendel Shtumpf, a moldy character actor suffering from aphasia and advanced catarrh, took the part he was born for, that of the drunken, addle-pated Czar Ahasuerus. In his fond distraction the Czar has been cuckolded by the buxom Czarina Vashti (played with a flushed exuberance and buoyant décolletage by the zaftig prima Hannah Muttelmessig), whose dalliance with her husband's spiritual advisor, the voluptuary monk Ratpukin, has become a national scandal. Ratpukin, portrayed by none other than Reb Hanover himself, is in fact the secret Jew Mordecai ben Kish in disguise. Having wormed his way into the Czar's confidence by alerting him to an assassination conspiracy, Mordecai, as Ratpukin, has been rewarded for his good offices by his elevation to the rank of *starets yurodiv*, or holy fool. He has also made himself indispensable to the Czarina, who is in thrall to him for the hypnotic powers she credits with having healed her son, the Czarevitch Oisip, a lifelong hemophiliac—played with a nervous intensity by Hershel Khevreman in his debut role. Through the mentor-like relationship he's established with the Czarevitch, the crypto-Jew has begun to indoctrinate the boy with contraband Jewish learning, which the precocious kid absorbs like a sponge. This strategy occasionally backfires, however, since young Oisip, unable to keep the sub rosa knowledge to himself, disgorges it at inopportune moments through a mouth as prodigal as his arteries in full hemorrhage. Thus does he threaten to blow Mordecai's cover.

Witness the scene in which, dining in her private apartments with the Czarina and her son, Ratpukin né Mordecai has begun to say a prayer of thanksgiving, when the boy interrupts.

Czarevitch Oisip (for which part Hershel is talcumed head to toe, giving his complexion a nearly albino cast): "You forgot to wash your hands, your worship, for it is written, 'When they go into the tent of meeting, they shall wash with water, that they die not.' We learn from this verse that whoever does not take care of this, and appears before the King with grubby hands, is punishable by death. For what reason? Because a man's hands dwell in the topmost part of the world. There is one finger on a man's hand that is the finger that Moses raised. For it is written, 'And you shall make bars of acacia wood: five bars for the boards of the one side of the tabernacle, and five bars for the boards of the other side of the tabernacle,' and then it is written . . . "

Ratpukin/Mordecai: "An extraordinary boy! A very angel of God!" Beaming through greasepaint as thick as cake frosting at the Czarina and her daughters, who sit in utter perplexity as the youth continues his drash.

The Czarevitch: " ... These five bars are called the five centuries, through which the Tree of Life passes, and the holy covenant of circumcision is effected through the five fingers of the hand ... "

Ratpukin/Mordecai, still extolling the boy's virtues, even as (with a "by your leave") he whacks the kid over the head with his slapstick to shut him up. Abruptly the Czarevitch starts to bleed, the blood spouting from the crown of his flaxen wig in a veritable geyser. (An effect cleverly engineered by the resourceful stage manager Zaynvel Traifnyak, employing a hose, a bilge pump, and a bucket of grenadine-tinctured kvass.) Flustered, the phony monk tries first to stopper the flow of blood with a bottle cork before remembering his hypnotic powers. He wriggles his fingers, incants some kabbalistic cantrip ("Shabiri, beriri, riri, ri—I am thirsty for water in white cups"), and the fountain of blood abates; the Czarina once again shows her gratitude by taking the false monk to her bosom—for he has advised her that the flesh is best subdued by an uninhibited surrender to its temptations.

All of this is observed from behind the wainscoting by the Czar's evil minister Haman—played by Gdalye Gruber, typecast as usual for his lizard's eyes in the shadow of their shaggy monobrow. Jealous of the *starets'* influence over the Czarina and incensed at the liaison's potential for compromising the state, Haman dutifully reports their antics to the Czar.

Haman: "You have been deceived by a *zhid* posing as a crackpot saint. He has infected your family with his obscenity and, worse, is using from the Czarevitch his blood to bake it in matzohs for his filthy Jew rituals. For this affront, I recommend you slaughter all the Jews in your kingdom."

The Czar, not unreceptive to the suggestion: "Aren't we killing them already as fast as we can?" For there had been much butchering of late.

Given leave to settle with the crypto-Jew in whatever manner he sees fit, Haman orders his creature (a putty-nosed Chaim Cholyerah) to poison the blintzes for which the Jew has a famous yen. When Mordecai has consumed at least a dozen with no ill effects, Haman then sends his minions into the Czarina's chambers, where the iron-constitutioned imposter is found frolicking with Vashti and her daughters to a gypsy violin. Seizing him in the face of the Czarina's protests, they drag him kicking across the courtyard and toss him down a well, firing pistol shots after him and flinging oaths to the effect that the rest of his race are soon to follow his lead. But when the thugs have departed, Mordecai, whom faith has made indestructible, crawls out over the rim of the well, still vital despite the water spurting through the sieve of his bullet-riddled cassock. Removing his long Ratpukin beard to scratch his own scraggly whiskers underneath, he resolves to save his endangered people.

In a rhyming soliloquy, accompanied by Feivish the Fiddle and Shmulik Trombone, Mordecai hatches a plot of his own. Safely assuming that his monopolizing of the Czarina's attentions has left Ahasuerus high and dry, he decides with his best pander's instincts to introduce the Czar to his "cousin" Esther. He begs an audience with the squiffy autocrat and lewdly suggests a rendezvous between Ahasuerus and the hot-blooded Esther, whose physical attributes he fulsomely praises, admitting of only one flaw.

"She has a speech impediment."

Ahasuerus: "So what I want a girl with a speech impediment? What kind enticement you call that?"

Mordecai, grinning slyly: "Her impediment is that she can't say no."

Enter Esther, played by the toothsome Mademoiselle Keni Hefker, displaying to generous advantage the same fetching proportions she peddles offstage to the highest bidder. She commences to tempt the Czar, allowing him to sample her charms with the promise of their full disclosure if he will first punish Haman for his treachery against the Jews.

Ahasuerus, suddenly unmindful of a long anti-Semitic tradition, inquires of the girl, "You're Jewish?" Then he proceeds to reverse all the discriminatory policies of his administration and has Haman hanged with swift dispatch. The Jews turn out en masse to dance a jig about the lynched minister, abusing his dangling corpse with their noise-making gragers. Esther rewards the Czar with an ecstatic night, practicing upon him all her professional wiles—the Akkadian plough, the Circassian monkey—which, while performed behind a backlit sheet with stylized acrobatics, still manage to put the audience in a ruttish sweat. When the scrim is removed Esther is seen stretching luxuriously in bed beside the deceased Ahasuerus, who has expired with a smile.

The final act culminates in Czarevitch Oisip's assumption of his father's vacated throne. In his fervor for the tradition of his mentor, who has at last abandoned his monkish masquerade, the Czar Designate has adopted the more *heimisheh* name of Farfel, and to make it official, he's also resolved to convert to the Jewish faith. The decision has been further prompted by his passion for the legacy of his dead father's mistress, Esther, whom he wishes to make his czarina. Thus, a grand public ceremony is staged, combining coronation, marriage, and circumcision. Beneath the wedding canopy Czar Farfel delivers his post-nuptial homily, an arcane and pedantic drash ("I do not fear the evil eye, because I am the son of a great and noble fish and fish do not fear the evil eye, for it is written: 'And let them swarm as a multitude in the midst of the earth.' So what does 'as a multitude' mean? It means . . . ") that has everyone yawning impatiently. Mordecai, the newly appointed Prime Minister, has also been engaged to perform the office of *mohel*; so rather than whack his protegé over the head with his slapstick, he takes up an outsize pair of scissors to clip the fledgeling Czar's putz—which, thanks to a papier-mâché replica sculpted by Zaynvl Traifnyak with affectionate attention to detail, is heroically engorged. The completed operation results in the Czar's spraying blood (once again the crimson kvass) in a surging trajectory, wielding the synthetic shwantz like a rampant firehose, while Mordecai declares that Moshiach Tseytn, the time of the Messiah, has arrived and all is permitted. Jews and gentiles alike cavort about the newlyweds, catching the ichor from the Czar's unruly member in kiddush cups, drinking their fill.

It was generally acknowledged among the Jews that a classic Purim shpiel ought to turn the world topsy-turvy; indeed, the audience was enjoined to get so drunk that they couldn't tell Haman from Mordecai, and even a soupçon of indecency was tolerated. For all that, most of the Drogobychers in attendance drew the line at the extremity of Hershel's play. Heresy aside, its transparent sendup of the times promised to make the shtetl's already precarious situation even more vulnerable. Of course there were youthful members of the audience who applauded the play's seditious content, though they objected to it at the same time on ideological grounds, complaining that the messianic age should be ushered in by Marx or Theodore Herzl rather than a Jewish despot. Arguing amongst themselves, they were shouted down by their pious elders, who claimed that the piece degraded humanity itself. With this opinion the impresario and director Elihu Hanover did not wholly disagree, though he insisted that controversy made good theater. But if the Jews were appalled, how much more so the Russian authorities, whom the *schutz-judn*, the informers, had made aware of the play's subversiveness. Before the local police were moved to action, however, the troupe, anticipating an inhospitable response, had already decamped. They fled to another province, where they performed the play again to similar outrage, but once more they managed to escape retribution, leaving behind them a trail of righteous indignation across Galicia and into the breadbasket countryside of the Ukrainian steppes.

That the Pishtipls had become in effect an outlaw company did not seem to bother Reb Hanover in the least, having as he did a taste for tastelessness and notoriety at any cost. This was Hershel's perception as he labored under the impresario's auspices to fashion another play, more scurrilous if possible than the previous. Apprenticed to the unorthodox old showman, he seemed to have surrendered wholeheartedly to his own evil intention, conceiving vehicles that increased the peril the troupe was already in. Nobody appeared to mind; on the contrary, the ragtag ensemble encouraged Hershel's immoderate efforts. Largely an assemblage of superannuated duffers and blowzy matrons with shady resumés, they seemed to welcome the opportunity to behave in public like devils on furlough from the abyss. Having found his voice, Hershel felt he had found a family as well. It was not an especially cozy family, since it had no fixed abode, and the unrepentant example of its members disqualified them from serving in loco parentis; nor did the ingénues in the company, with their aggressively come-hither ways, inspire the chaste affection of siblings. But while Hershel did on occasion succumb to virtually incestuous relations with some of the ladies—when their bodies weren't otherwise employed as a medium of exchange—he mostly abstained, his celibacy helping to stoke the yearning that in turn fueled his theatrical conceits. And onstage, inhabiting the variety of roles he assigned himself (lover, madman, saint, and fool), Hershel was truly at home. Meanwhile the Pishtipl Players somehow managed to stay one step ahead of the law, which they eluded thanks to the wily contrivances of their director, who led them on a zigzag circuit throughout the Pale of Settlement with the authority of a patriarch.

There was more to come, much more. There was, for instance, the town of Zlotopol, where the pavements were foundered fence planks sunken in mud and nature a lone linden tree; and in the market, orientally noisy with shmeiklers, peddlers, and black marketeers, Elijah sold a rabbit skin into which he'd sewn a living tabby cat. Why, Hershel wondered, did the prophet, who possessed supernatural powers, constantly resort to such churlish tricks? But he had no time to ponder the conundrum, since the rabbit had meowed in the hands of its purchaser, who began to raise a hue and cry. Then Elijah and Hershel made tracks—the old man hitching the skirts of his caftan to hoof it on drumstick shanks—never pausing till they reached the margins of that huddled town, where they took shelter in a cathedral-size haybarn. The barn must have served a double function, for there were theatrical properties of an Old Testament character in storage there: a bargeboard crate bedizened with paste baubles representing a portable Ark of the Covenant, a staff sprouting rubber serpents twined caduceus-fashion that signified Aaron's rod, a fabric and wattle-ribbed Leviathan, a frightwig simulating Samson's unkempt mane. There was a mean wooden ladder leaning against the hayloft that made no claims to mythical provenance, which Elijah nevertheless insisted was the same ladder the patriarch Jacob had long ago seen thronged with angels; and while Hershel had been deceived once too often by the scapegrace prophet to believe anything he said, he still followed the old man (it had become his helpless habit) up the ladder to the loft, where they might bunk for the night. Velvl Sfparb, though nearly spent, wanted to describe to the widow the unearthly radiance that Hershel saw emanating from the loft, but the train, which had slowed to a crawl, finally came to a screeching stop, causing the few passengers still left standing to sprawl on top of one another.

There was a moment when the dank walls of the cattle car were striped with a platinum light; then the door was unbolted, and the light that had at first just seeped now deluged the compartment. Velvl had the impression that he and the other passengers were being flushed from the car in that flood of light, though the process was much facilitated by shouts of "Juden, heraus!", by kicks, whips, and rifle butts. Then they were marooned on a concrete island under arc lights whose stupefying brilliance penetrated the mist and heightened the clarity of the scene to a cinematic unreality. Stare long enough and the pandemonium surrounding them might begin to come true, but they were blessedly forbidden the privilege of gawking; they had no time to catch the breeze that relieved the suffocation of the freight car, harried as they were up the ramp by barking soldiers and wraiths in striped pajamas with comic hats like fallen soufflés. The wraiths encircled them as in a *mitzvah tants* to relieve them of their belongings—wresting suitcases, sewing machines, and featherbeds from their grasp, rifling pockets and fingering orifices for hidden heirlooms—which they immediately began to sort into their respective piles. The guards in belted green jackets with helmets like phallus heads shouted oaths and inflicted random beatings; the soldiers in black with gold piping, death's heads adorning their caps and lightning bolts on their lapels, themselves whip-thin, uncoiled bullwhips like striking cobras. A standing orchestra, whose mismatched rags were distinguished by white paper dickies, stood in a kiosk playing sentimental lieder while assaulted by darting bats. There was a sickly acrid odor imbued with a hint of cinnamon that singed the nostrils, a tethered airship buoyed like a floating torpedo above a looming pillar of flame.

In the corners of Velvl's eyes, which only flickeringly communicated with his brain, he was aware that the wraiths and green soldiers were in the process of culling the living from the dead. It was a somewhat arbitrary task: the dead, or at least those perceived to be, were tossed helter-skelter onto growling lorries whose beds lay level with the platform that also served as a loading dock; while those perceived to be yet alive were goaded into the heaving current of stumblers and staggerers, their tongues extended like snails' heads to catch the moisture in the air. For many, however, the categories of quick or dead did not seem to apply, and these marginal creatures, most of them children, wandered gibbering beneath the haloed reflectors until they were dispatched by an efficient Luger or clubbed to bonemeal. Amid the howling of victims and persecutors, the shouts of "Schweinedreck!" and "Schweinerei!", could be heard distinct commands in approximate Yiddish: "Men to the left, women and children to the right!" Velvl fell in among the ranks of men lumbering five abreast, traversing a gauntlet of curses mitigated here and there by a death's head officer wielding a clipboard, pronouncing in tones of arch assurance: "Keine Angst." Velvl thought he preferred the shouts. Somewhere behind him in the stygian darkness beyond the railroad spur was the past, where experience had once been rumored to matter. But as his memory seemed to have deserted him and the present was seething with fiends sewn from dragons' teeth, Velvl was hard pressed to find reasons for maintaining his flagging consciousness.

Though consciousness persisted, and as he trudged up the farflung ramp among the stolid others, Velvl glimpsed, in the adjacent ranks of women, one from whose arms dangled a spindly, bug-eyed little girl. Then the child was torn from the mother's arms and carried like a defective manikin across the platform, where she was flung atop the tangled heap of bodies in a truckbed, while the hysterical woman fell to her knees in the thickening mist. A dog, snarling through the open cage of its wire muzzle, was bidden to attack her, tearing along with the fabric of her dress the scant flesh from the angle of her hip. Uninvited, a vintage saying invaded Velvl's head: "When the dogs howl, the Angel of Death has come to town; when the dogs frolic, Elijah is around." He had an impulse to call out to the woman, but was abruptly thrust forward in line, where he found himself face to face with a dashing death's head officer, a superman twirling a swagger stick in his leather-gloved hand.

"Jahre?" asked the officer in a German the austere second cousin to Velvl's own *mameloshen*. Beside the officer, who was doubtless a commandant, stood an interpreter from the tribe of zebra-striped haftlings, saying needlessly, "Your age?"

When Velvl took a moment to consider, the commandant left off admiring his own dexterity with his baton to inquire, "Verstanden?" "Farshteyst?" asked the interpreter.

Confusing his age in years with the age in which he lived, Velvl replied in all sincerity, "A finster yor, di farkucktzeytn." Where the words came from, he couldn't have said, unless a *dybbuk* had gotten hold of his tongue.

The interpreter repeated Velvl's answer as best he could: "Die Scheissepoche, the age of shit," for which he received a cuff from the swagger stick. Then, interested, the commandant cocked a brow, allowing his monocle to fall out of his eye and dangle from its ribbon at his decorated breast. The mist had begun to leak dollops of rain that pelted the taut umbrella the wraith had opened above his master's head, as Velvl braced himself for the inevitable battery—so be it. But instead of assaulting the impertinent prisoner, the officer stretched the corners of his mouth in a tight-lipped, pickerel smile. Leaning forward as if he had all the time in the world, as if the untold numbers were not awaiting his examination and verdict, he lifted Velvl's chin with his baton and inquired in an urbane voice, "Beruf?" Cuffed again, the wraith uttered a sullen, "Parnoss? Livelihood?"

Without hesitating this time, Velvl declared, "Dertzayler."

Said the interpreter at a questioning glance from the commandant, "Dichter." Storyteller.

The answer caused the commandant to unzipper his thin lips, showing perfect teeth. "Du musst versprechen später mir ein Märchen zu erzählen?" "Later you will perhaps tell me a story?" the interpreter grudgingly submitted to Velvl, as the commandant spun his baton again. When it came to rest in his fingers, the crop end was pointing in the direction of the tributary of men deferred from oblivion (for the whispered asides of the wraiths had advised them of what they already knew). Velvl realized that his cheek had won him a temporary reprieve: he was being channeled toward the barracks instead of the chimneys. He remembered a story about a legendary Persian Jewess called Sarah haZad, who had forestalled her execution at the hands of a sultan by beguiling him with endless tales. Velvl imagined he might do the same over time with the commandant, spellbinding him for however long it took the approaching enemy (there must be an approaching enemy) to break through the German lines and liberate the camp.

And then . . . But seeing how the swollen stream designated as human detritus had begun to bear away the childless woman, Velvl bit down hard on his tongue; his gnashed teeth nearly met in the middle of that powdery appendage, whose tip, not quite separated from the rest, remained hanging like a berry from a stem. He somehow managed to suppress a cry of pain as his mouth filled with blood, then coughed explosively, spraying the spit-polished boots of the death's head commandant.

The officer looked at his sullied boots, which the now steady rain had already begun to wash clean, and sighed. "Was denke ich? Hier enden alle Geschichte . . ." "What am I thinking? This is the place where all stories end," said the interpreter almost simultaneously, stating the new directive with obvious zeal: "Forget the detour, Herr Scheissemensch, you deserve that you should reach your destination without further delay." Then one of the boots he had bloodied hastened Velvl's reconvergence into the sluggish multitude.

He pressed his way forward among the aged and infirm, their empty jaws working like insects' mandibles, groped past the blind man spilling blood from a severed ring finger and the dwarf hiding his head beneath a pregnant lady's indifferent skirts. Past a charred stick maiden clutching the barbed wire fence beneath a sign like a pirate flag, her hair still smoldering. Where the turreted gates swung open to admit them, he stepped over a bloated infant whose belly had burst like a melon, shoved aside a genderless specter with translucent skin, and trod an empty vial of poison under foot, until he reached her—at least he believed it was her, though his eyes were poor and the rain was becoming torrential. He grabbed hold of her clammy hand and squeezed it tight, feeling a corresponding sensation envelop his heart. Speaking with a limp that was the verbal complement to her favoring of her own wounded leg, he informed her, "Elijah too would stand like the monocled commandant at the crossroads, directing traffic, sending to heaven the righteous and the sinners to Gehenna . . ." For speaking out of turn he was awarded the stroke of a lash across his back, its sting sounding in his ears like a vaudevillian's slapstick.

When finally she turned toward him, hair streaking her forehead like seaweed, the widow greeted Velvl with a look of unalloyed terror—the kind of look he supposed the Angel of Death himself must have been accustomed to receiving from his victims. Nevertheless, buffeted by the storm, he continued his story.

There was the night the Pishtipl Players performed their latest production in Reb Zalman Rappaport's haybarn, which they'd commandeered on account of a downpour of biblical proportions that had made a lagoon of the market square. This was in the Byelorussian town of Zlotopol. The barn's interior, under a leaky roof upon which the storm beat a steady tattoo, was lit by eerie green lights from benzine-soaked burlap and hissing naphtha flares. Sleeping children hung from the rafters in swaying bassinets as if cradled in pelicans' beaks; sweating flystrips dangled in spirals like shorn *peyos* curls. From the horse stalls the orchestra played instruments that repeated the gabbling and honking of the drenched turkeys and geese in the yard. The crowd about the makeshift stage—planks mounted on waterlogged hay bales nibbled by goats—were a diverse lot of herring peddlers, patch tailors, merchants in frock coats, porters in short jerkins drinking mead from earthen tankards, their wives in babushkas slathering horseradish on sausages. Rowdy to begin with, they grew increasingly hostile and bewildered as the play progressed.

The Pishtipls were performing Hershel Khevreman's most recent offering, entitled "King Yoyzl," which detailed the history of the false messiah Yoyzl Baalguf, who preaches a gospel of redemption through sin. Yoyzl, played by Hershel himself, is a character of mercurial moods that fluctuate between a cringing humility and an arrogant self-aggrandizement encouraged by his fanatic disciple Rabbi Zimzum. (The zealot Zimzum was portrayed by Reb Hanover, who enacted a double role, appearing alternately as a dissolute prophet Elijah.) In an inflated mood Yoyzl has adorned the Torah scrolls in intimate female

apparel—a whalebone corset, a nainsook peignoir—
with the express intention of having relations with the
Word itself on Shabbos Eve, according (as he claims)
to divine prescription. "In the sabbatical year of the
7th millenium," declares the charlatan, "which by my
calculations begins tonight, the Torah sheds its material
garment for one of pure spirituality." Then before a
minyan composed of his brainwashed followers, which
include an offkey cantor (Gdalye Gruber) and a doting
personal scribe (Mendel Shtumpf), he begins to divest
the Torah, delicately, of its diaphanous garments. He
stretches the naked scrolls across an artificial altar,
removes the silk gartel from his waist, and drops his
moleskin trousers to expose his hairy nates; then he
prepares to lie prostrate upon holy writ. It was at this
point, when the crowd itself had had enough, hurling
salvos of rotten vegetables and fishheads at the stage,
that the barn doors burst open, admitting a squadron of
armed regulars from the local barracks, some of them
on thunderous horseback.

Alerted to the disreputable proceedings in Zalman
Rappaport's haybarn, they had come to close down
the temporary theater and arrest the players, whose
buffoonery (of a peculiarly vulgar *zhid* strain) was
in defiance of the laws of God and man. And if the
audience should get in the way of the performance of
their duty, then the audience got what it deserved.

Chaos reigned as the soldiers laid into the crowd
with flailing truncheons, dragoons trampling the odd
citizen or player under their horses' hooves. Some

of the Pishtipls—notably a nimble-fingered Chaim Cholyerah and Zaynvel Traifnyak—took advantage of the wholesale panic to fleece a pocket or two, even as they were themselves in flight. A few of the ingenues flung their skirts over their heads in a burlesque of fright, shaking their flounced drawers in the faces of their attackers—which had the effect of causing even the most murderous soldiers to miss a beat in their bludgeonings. Under cover of the commotion, Reb Hanover, dressed in the Bedouin rags of an incarnate Elijah—come to herald the true messiah, he'd been seduced by the false—adjured his apprentice, still buttoning his flies, to follow him up a rickety ladder to the hayloft. It seemed an impractical escape route to Hershel, but as the soldiers were already at their heels, he began a mad scramble up the ladder behind the impresario. When he reached the top, Reb Hanover, as Elijah, hauled Hershel the remaining few feet into the loft, where the playwright was momentarily stunned by a platinum radiance. He turned back blinking toward the ladder in time to witness a minor miracle: every rung that the soldier in pursuit was ascending collapsed beneath the tread of his heavy boots. In consequence, just as he attained the top of the ladder, with no footholds left to support him the soldier slid back to the bottom, yowling as the palms of his hands collected splinters along the way. (After which the ladder struts, no longer joined by rungs, toppled to either side like an abandoned pair of stilts.) Then Hershel turned around again toward the brightness, which, when his eyes began to adjust, revealed Reb Zalman's loft to have both much and nothing in common with anyplace on earth.

"Welcome to paradise," greeted the old reprobate prophet.

Replied Hershel, thinking this was perhaps the cruelest trick that Elijah had yet to play on him: "But I'm not dead yet."

"Who says?"

Casting about him, Hershel saw that they had mounted another stage, a more clarified version of the one they'd escaped below, for while this one was not much larger than the original, it seemed at the same time to contain a world. The façade of the prayerhouse was as slapdash as the one Zaynvl Traifnyak had painted for "King Yoyzl," the houses along the switchback street just as skewed and unplumb, their windows crooked, walls slanted, roof shingles curling like Keni Hefker's fake lashes. But though nothing was rendered in more than two paltry dimensions, the off-kilter design of the shtetlscape spawned echoes that suggested an extra dimension of frozen music and cunning arabesques. The standard materials—rude stucco, timber, and thatch—intimated other more precious textures, just as the oil canisters and poppyseed cakes in a shop window, the pyramid of cabbages in a market stall, hinted at having secret lives. An onion dome, a wedding canopy, a samovar, all corresponded to other shapes unimagined (concluded Hershel) by the minds of men, and even the smells—delicatessen, dishwater, kerosene—were distilled into a collective ambrosia. The beaten carpets, airing in open windows, were illuminations for sacred texts, the goosedown, drifting in the atmosphere, feathers from angels' wings. Simultaneously familiar and strange, it was a scene that, under an array of stars as relentless as floods, seemed to duplicate the hidden configurations of Hershel's own brain, but still it failed to convince him. Nothing in heaven appeared to be natural, or for that matter even credible, at least not to the naked eye of the living.

By the same token the costumed population, strolling to and fro across the boards, failed in their spectral outlines to achieve the authenticity of mortals. Lacking substance, they passed through Hershel like cobwebs sweeping over his face and limbs. Upstaged by the resonant architecture, they seemed conspicuous only for their absence of any essential matter and, in Hershel's judgment, also a little lost. To distinguish himself from their shadowless promenade, he pinched his arm with a will, until he'd determined that he could still bleed. But while the dead had perhaps yet to come into their own (or was it that Hershel needed years to appreciate their solidity?), there were other beings that looked perfectly at home in Kingdom Come. Though diminutive, they stole the spotlight from the deceased by their sheer corporeal presence, posing on imaginary eaves and ledges, flocking atop gables like finials, outnumbering the leaves of trees. Most appeared to be species of rare birds, others unusual breeds that bore some native resemblance to ferrets, vipers, jackals, and chimpanzees. There were hybrids: part rodent, say, and part electric eel, miniature basilisks, lunar hares, and manticores, compact mythical beasts that gave the impression of anticipating some breathless event.

Among them, seated on the skeletal sail of a windmill revolving leisurely at the edge of the stage, Hershel spotted a tiny monkey—with no expertise in the subject, he thought it must be a spider monkey— with the face of a sad old man. Even in the midst of so many oddities, this one looked misplaced, though its familiarity to the playwright bespoke a certain imperative. Rather than return his sense of recognition, however, the thing seemed to be actively ignoring Hershel, though he still wasn't fooled. When the red sail dipped in its next creaking revolution, he lunged forward to snatch the animal from its perch, hugging it to his aching breast. The pressure against his heart released a torrent of emotions, among them a passionate affection for the trembling creature and a conviction that, for all its surface allure, paradise was not his element after all. Head spinning, Hershel shut his eyes and saw before him a twirling compass needle, which pointed now toward the terrestrial, now the celestial, now the real and now the make-believe. Then even as Elijah, changed into a functionary's tailcoat, tapped his shoulder to whisper, "God wants a word with you," Hershel tucked his fugitive soul under his arm and, bolting toward the edge of the loft, leaped into the darkness beyond.

He landed with a thump face-down in the sweaty bed, bereft of clothing, his back and shoulders covered in cupping globes like a glass harmonica. The mattress, though damp, was warm, as were the steamy cups, and Hershel, nestled as he was in the bosom of the world, had never felt so serene. When he opened his eyes, there was the crone standing over him, but instead of inspiring fear or disgust, she appeared, in her rustic *shmattes*, relatively benign, chewing her lip in a hushed solicitude. Heaving a sigh that emitted a peaceful whimper, Hershel decided he ought to reassure her. He began through a slow evolution to raise himself to a seated position, the unstuck cups rolling from his back like scales from a dinosaur's spine. Deliciously giddy, he made no effort to hide his nakedness—it never occurred to him he should feel embarrassed. Then he was on his feet and wobbling, his legs not yet fully operative, so that he had to be supported by the old woman's sinewy arms. He gratefully returned her embrace, feeling through her weskit and skirts the contours of a body surprisingly supple, whose pungent proximity provoked a stirring in his loins. Sensing his excitement, the hag let out a cackle and Hershel laughed as well, kissing in his lightheaded exuberance her cracked lips and crannied cheeks. She cackled again when her flesh adhered to Hershel's own lips like bits of taffy. He spat them out, wiping the salty remnant from his tongue with the back of his hand; then, gingerly, he touched the sapless features of her face and began to trace with his fingertips the crusted distortions of her forehead, cheeks, and chin—at which he proceeded to pull. Whiskers, bumps, and wens came away from her bones like sticking plasters, the false flesh peeling from the real in mucilaginous strands, until he'd denuded her face of the last vestiges of its grotesque mask to reveal the comely girl beneath.

"Salka?" asked Hershel, lifting the ragmop of her wig off over her midnight hair.

The girl beamed, shaking out the lush serpentine curls, "Tahkeh, who else?" Then she explained, "My reputation as *vildeh moid*, a naughty girl, it marked me, so I had to disguise myself. I became old Malka, the healer woman. It wasn't a bad life. I knew you would happen along eventually."

"You saved me," said Hershel, while his longlost beloved plucked the remaining cups from his back as if popping corks and told him he shouldn't make such a thing of it. Salvation had become her stock in trade. At length they fell into the former sickbed, festooned with medicinal herbs, and made love, and afterwards Hershel announced that he too had found his vocation.

"I'm a playwright."

"Then," said Salka, unaccustomed to mincing words, "you must go to America and ply your trade." Yiddish theater, she had him to know, was all the rage in America.

Hershel thought it over. "Will you come with me?"

So they dressed, packed some food for the journey in a carpet bag, and set off down the road in the noonday sun toward the border and the border after that. Along the way they cautioned each other to keep looking to the horizon, beyond which was the sea, rather than be distracted by *ganefs* or bureaucrats demanding improbable papers and reports of murdered archdukes.

At the outset Salka had suggested they take a shortcut across a meadow through a glade of locust trees, in the middle of which they came upon a supine youth. Stooping beside his marmoreal body, Hershel turned out his own empty pockets, then asked Salka if she could spare a couple of coins to place over his eyes— his azure eyes that had so far been spared by carrion crows. The girl, demonstrating a practical side that was becoming ever more manifest, insisted that they must be prudent—the New World would exact a toll. Then she leaned over the dead soldier herself, and Hershel wondered for an instant if she might try to resurrect him, but instead she removed the cold pistol from his hand, closed his lids with her fingers, and pressed a pellet of unleavened dough against his brow. This last was to plug up the hole in his head, lest some vagabond soul enter there to disturb his rest.

TITLES IN THE COMPANION SERIES
THE ART OF THE NOVELLA

THE ART OF THE NOVELLA

THE CONTEMPORARY ART OF THE NOVELLA